INTRODUCTION

Let me introduce myself, my name is at the start of my first case.
'**The Serial Killers Secret**' was Inspector Peter Stewart. Now chief inspector. 45yrs, 5ft-10in tall, slim, black hair and divorced. Helen Stewart is my ex and her mother, who I partly hold responsible for the marriage from hell, is Audrey Allard. You will see that I still want to make Audrey pay.

Constable Forward is a very close friend, in fact we really like each other's company. 33yrs old, Jet-black hair, slim, about my height and very determined in all she does. She has looks as well as brains.

Sergeant Jack Taylor, a long serving and honest as the day is long, he is someone you can trust in all matters. 6ft tall, he is well-built and 40yrs old. Jack had been passed over for promotion three times, but now our chief

Sergeant Sid Kemp, he is the desk sergeant, always playing pranks on the rest of us but a nice man. Stocky and only 5ft tall and has been 37yrs old for the last 7yrs.

Sergeant Ted Reed looks after the cells, a quite man, approx 6ft tall and medium build. He is only 41yrs old but looks older as he is going grey.

Sergeant Green. His nickname 'BULLDOZER' is due to his approach to violent criminals. 6ft 4in of bulging muscle, is very comforting on raids.

Constable Arnold. His nickname 'MAMMOTH' is due mainly to his bulk, unlike Sergeant Green he is 5ft 11in tall but 17 stone. Both Green and Arnold unbelievably, are quite gentle men, both turn into raging hulks of fury when confronted by violence.

Constable Brenda Sky. Slim, very pretty with long blond hair. She is 29yrs old, very keen but not always thorough in her job.

Constable Bart White. He teams up with Constable Sky and often takes her on dates. He is blonde, 30yrs old and like Sky still learning.

1st case= 'THE SERIAL KILLERS SECRET'
Victims poisoned are all legal people.
2nd case= 'ACCUSED FALSELY' a handbag with supernatural powers its aim justice.
3rd case= = 'STRONG EVIDENCE' exactly what the title states
4th case=='THE ELUSIVE VIGILANTE' and no motives for the murders?
Follow the characters lives as I tell you of the third and fourth cases

JAMES M DYET

STRONG EVIDENCE

CASE 3

STRONG EVIDENCE

My name is Chief Inspector Peter Stewart. This case nearly made me lose faith in the British legal system.

I had just dropped my fiancée Gracie Day back at her shop after a lovely meal at her favourite restaurant, I thought I would treat her as she was always cooking me meals. It was only 8pm but she needed an early night, she had to be up early for the builders who wanted to start her new kitchen at 7.30am.

After a coffee and a cuddle, I set off home to watch a new DVD I had bought.
With the DVD in the player and my feet up, I felt lovely and relaxed. What more could I ask? My flask of black coffee, packet of cashew nuts and ice cream with blueberry yoghurt poured over it.

Twenty minutes into the film, I had finished the ice cream and about to finish a packet of cashew nuts when the phone rang. Typical, as soon as I get engrossed in a film, I get interrupted. Reluctantly I paused the DVD and answered the phone. To my surprise, it was one of my oldest friends, William Baker, whom I hadn't seen or heard from for over 7yrs.

I forgot myself and called him by his nickname Monk, the reason was when we were young he always wore his duffle coat and kept his hood up.

William knew I was an inspector in the police force and wanted my help. His brother Alistair has been arrested for murder. He claims he is innocent but his guilt seems overwhelming due to the evidence.

After agreeing to look into why his brother was charged and telling him not to worry, I made notes then I finished watching my film.

I phoned the desk sergeant Sid Kemp to find out who was in charge of the case. I had been on a fortnight's holiday and been out of touch with the yard. Sid informed me that Inspector Carol Forward was in charge of the case. Feeling a bit sick at making a bit of a pig of my self, I took a couple of indigestion tablets and retired to my bed, as soon as my head hit the pillow to my relief I was out for the count.

The next morning as my eyelids forced themselves open to let the outside world in and bring me back to reality, all I could think about was savouring a nice cup of tea and perhaps a couple of oat biscuits. Funny thing is, for the last fortnight I had had no trouble waking up, as this was my first day returning to work the effort was immense. As I passed the telephone, I spotted the notes I had written down about Williams Brother, I was suddenly intrigued and my energy flooded back, my hand shot forward to the phone and dialled to meet Carol Forward about the case.

Back at the station, Carol and I grabbed a coffee each and sat down to discuss the case.   The victim was a young woman in her thirties. Someone had shot her through the heart at close range on the 22nd of this month.

"What evidence have you obtained to make an arrest on Mr. Alistair Baker?"

"Apparently he had been visiting Kelly Hope; they had a big bust up and a blazing argument over another man on the 8th that was a fortnight before her murder."

"You can't formally arrest someone on a suspicion, unless you have evidence."

"You have a habit of interrupting Peter, the gun was found beside the body and Baker's fingerprints were all over it, funny thing is he never seemed to mind us taking his prints, in fact he seemed eager for us to take them to prove his innocence."

"I take it he never had an alibi for the time of the murder?"

"He told us he had had an operation a week before her murder and was resting in bed. That was what the argument was about as he imagined she would see the other man while he was out of the way."

"The operation was a week after the blazing argument so why wait until after the operation? Surly if he was that jealous he would have shot her before going into hospital. Another thing that doesn't add up is why leave the gun at the murder scene with your finger prints on it."

"Baker had his appendix out on the 16th and apparently he would have still been very sore. That would back up his alibi that he was recuperating but we have to go on the facts."

"Have you interviewed the other man involved with Kelly Hope?"

"The man concerned is Trevor Thompson and he was working his shift at the hospital on the evening she was shot."

"The hospital is only 5mins away from her flat, if the gun hadn't got baker's prints on it he could have been a suspect."

"Why are you trying to convince me Baker is innocent? Everything points to him, the blazing argument, jealously, prints on the gun and no alibi."

"That's the problem, it's all been handed to us on a plate, plus according to his brother he doesn't own a car. Baker lives over three miles away from Miss Hopes Flat. Even with pain killers he would be a bit stupid to go out that night in the cold."

"How could you have talked to his brother? Is there something you're not telling me about this case?"

"William Baker is an old friend and he phoned me last night, he filled me in on the case and his brother swears he is innocent."

"Perhaps you would like to work on this case with me? providing you're not emotionally evolved."

"No; William is just an old friend, I said I would try and get to the truth, I would like to talk to the accused if that's ok?"

"Anything to get to the truth, like I said you're officially on the case with me."

Sergeant Reed took us to Alistair's cell but he was fast asleep, the police doctor had given him an injection due to an infection in his wound, also a sedative to help with the pain.

"Thank you sergeant, I think we will leave Mr. Baker till the morning and perhaps he would be better in hospital, not in a chilli cell?"

"I did suggest that to the doctor but he ignored it, unless his hearing is impaired due to his attitude towards criminals."

"It's up to you Carol whether he goes into hospital, perhaps constables Sky and White could follow the ambulance and guard him for the night."

"I totally agree he hasn't been found guilty yet so let's go with your plan Peter and get him to hospital."

"Should I inform the chief about this or leave you to inform him?"

"Leave it to us Ted, you could phone for an ambulance while we round up Brenda Sky and Bart White."

"Do you know if Trevor Thompson is working tonight Carol?"

"Yes he is, every night this week according to him, I don't think you will like him."

"The way I see it is, if he hadn't been messing about with Baker's girl she would still be alive, still it takes two I suppose."

"By the way Peter, the gun used was stolen 5 months ago from a Colonel Samson during a break-in at his country house, he was in hospital at the time."

"Let's get to the hospital and have a word with this Mr. Thompson, Carol."

We found him trying to chat up one of the nurses, he tried to get fresh and got a slap round the face, he went to slap her back but Inspector Forward rushed to him and put him in an arm lock forcing him against the wall.

The nurse refused to press charges of indecent assault. Carol released him and told him we needed to ask more questions about Kelly Hope's murder.

"You like hitting women do you Thompson? How about we go outside and see what you are really made of." I said as memories flooded back to when my father struck my mother.

"Calm down chief and just ask your questions."

"Get lost I'm not telling that mad man anything." Thompson ranted at Carol.

"In that case, get your coat your coming down to the station and you can stay there till you do answer my questions." I said as my blood started to boil.

"Ok what do you want to know? I have already told the lady everything."

"Miss Hope rejected your advances didn't she and you couldn't stand that could you, Is that why you murdered her?"

"You have your murderer, leave me alone or I will make an official complaint."

"Come on Peter let's go, I would like a word with you."

We made our way back to the car and once inside she let rip.

"What do you think you're playing at? Any more outbursts and your off the case, all the evidence points to Alistair Baker."

"Call it what you like, gut feeling, intuition or just a bad feeling, he is involved in this up to his neck and I will work it out."

"I don't see how you can but providing you take control of your temper we will work on it together."

"I am sorry Carol, you're a real gem, if I hadn't fell for Gracie we could have been good together, it's your case so I will consult you on everything I do."

"I haven't been completely honest with you about Thompson. 18 months ago, he tried to borrow some money from his mother, she refused and he put her in hospital. I was alerted at the time by a nurse, she was suspicious. His mother told the hospital she tripped over her Hoover. The injuries were consistent of blows to the face and shoulders. I followed it up and their immediate neighbour heard him shouting threats at his mother before the ambulance arrived."

"I can't in my wildest nightmares imagine anyone doing that to their own mother. Look the ambulance has just arrived with Alistair Baker. I must warn constables White and Sky to keep Thompson away from Baker."

Afterwards I suggested we talk to some of the late Miss Hope's neighbours even although Carol, Sky and White had already called on a few and got statements.

As Miss Hope had lived on the sixth floor, they had only visited the residents on the seventh, sixth, fifth, fourth and third floors for any information but without success. In my experience, the ground floor was the ears and eyes of visitors so off we went to the murder scene, '**Red Brick court.**'

There were four flats per floor and flat one was out, flat two was so high on drugs he was on another planet. Flat three was a rear flat and occupied by a dear old lady wearing a hearing aid that gave out a continual whistle, so after adjusting it for her we went on to flat four. A grumpy old man who seemed all bitter and twisted with the world opened the door, he stood there in his string vest and worn braces holding his grubby old trousers up, he suggested we talk to the nosey old bat in flat five on the first floor. How the other residents put up with his attitude and the smell of his smoking escaped me. His cigarette smoke had oozed round the edge of his front door turning his white doorframe brown, even the hall and stairwells stank of stale nicotine.

The old misery guts was right about flat five, she remembered Thompson mainly because he would look up at her sitting at her window and stick his two fingers up at her. Mrs Hilda Lewis was indeed the jewel in the crown of neighbourhood watch, not only did she note the times he called at the flat but took photos of his rude gestures.

My excitement vanished when she told us she had not seen him the day Miss Hope was shot. I took a note of the dates and times of Thompson's visits and tried the other flats.

No one in the other flats had seen either of the men that day only the residents that lived in that block of flats.

When things are not going well I get a mad craving for chocolate. I popped into the shop opposite the flats and bought a couple of bars. I have never seen a woman shovel chocolate down like Inspector Forward. In fact, she had finished hers before I was half way through mine. Just as I was going to drive away from the shop, I noticed a CCTV camera pointing our way in the shop. Hoping to get footage of that fateful evening I went back in, only to find the shopkeeper wipes the tape the next day if nothing happened on the day before.

Things certainly look bad for Baker and if we can't get a breakthrough, he will go down for the murder.

"Tell me Carol, what is Thompson's job in the hospital exactly?"

"I think he is at everybody's beckon call, he takes things from the wards to the lab for testing, wheels patients about, that sort of thing."

"What about wheeling patients to and from the operating theatre?"

"That would be part of his duties but he hasn't tried to do Baker any harm."

"Don't you understand, while Baker was still unconscious in the recovery room, Thompson could have taken the gun with him and pressed Bakers hand on the gun?"

"Well done Peter but how can you prove it, I'm afraid the courts go mainly on fact like evidence, not because you dislike someone. Best get back to the station and do our reports, then call it a day."

I was so sure Thompson was involved, I had a job getting to sleep as the thought did cross my mind I could be wrong. The motive must have been jealousy over Kelly but why kill her? Unless jealously or rejection was not the motive, if indeed he was rejected.

After a while, I finally dropped off to sleep. I was abruptly woken by my alarm clock at 6am. The temptation to silence it and sink into my pillow took all my will power not to become one with my bed.

Reluctantly I vacated my warm comfortable bed and made my way down to the kitchen. Two cups of tea later and I was still fighting to keep awake. My eyes felt heavy and they portrayed the kitchen through a white hazy cobweb. Rest my eyes for a minute was my answer, I let my eye lids close in slow motion until all light had been extinguished and my head slowly rested on the table.

Next thing I knew there was a loud banging on the back door, which abruptly brought me back to life. There peering through the back door window was a very concerned Inspector Forward. I rose up and opened the back door.

"What do you think you are playing at? Its 9.40am, I thought you were dead slumped over the table, what is wrong?

"Been awake most of the night, what if I am wrong and Baker did murder the girl? We have enough on Baker to convict him and nothing on Thompson."

"Don't worry, he will have a fair trial, if he is innocent the court will see justice is done. Come on get yourself upstairs and have a shower, you have 15mins to get down here, or I will be up."

"To think I wanted to marry you, I had a narrow escape, thanks to Gracie."

"If you don't hurry up I will show you what you missed, then you will wish you had picked me, so move it."

For a fleeting moment, I tingled from head to toe, as her fiery seductive eyes sparkled at me in a beckoning way. Just then, Gracie's face flashed in front of my eyes and with a smile, I rushed upstairs feeling even closer to Grace. As I was getting dressed, I heard Carol's mobile phone ring, next the sound of footsteps on their way up the stairs. Without knocking, Carol burst into the bedroom, she was red in the face and looking worried.

"It's the chief, something has happened to Gracie Day."

I felt a crushing pain in my chest as tears waited to flood from my eyes. As I took the mobile from her, I feared the worst; I listened as dread filled my brain.

"Don't worry Peter she will be ok, she is just shaken up and has a couple of bruises. Constable Arnold has accompanied her to the hospital so make your way there and put Inspector Forward back on."

Like one of those speeded up old movies I got dressed. Carol closely followed me as I headed out to the landing.

"Chief told me I have to stick to you like glue, mainly in case you do something stupid, which is why no one else will work with you."

I stopped for a second then as I rushed downstairs and shouted back.

"What are you not telling me Carol? Has someone attacked her?"

I turned and looked at her waiting for an answer; a stupid grin appeared on her face as she said.

"Let your mother in-law sort them out, no need for you to get done for G.B.H."

Without a word, I turned and left by the back door closely followed by Carol who took my car keys out of my hand and pointed to her car.

We never spoke all the way to the hospital, and no! I was not annoyed at her joke she was just trying to cheer me up.

As we pulled up outside the hospital I gave her a peck on the cheek, she smiled and gave my hand a squeeze before heading into the hospital.

"There is Constable Arnold over there outside that cubicle."

Carol said as she grabbed my arm. We quickly made our way over to get some answers and for me eager to comfort Grace. Constable Arnold beckoned us away from the cubicle, as he wanted to talk to us.

"Before you tear off round the corridors of the hospital looking for Thompson, he had nothing to do with it."

"What are you talking about constable? Tell me what happened."

"Miss Day was up early this morning, she was sorting some stock out in the shop. About 6.10am there was a knock on the door, she thought it was the milkman and opened the door, 2 youths pushed her out of the way and luckily, she landed on some empty cardboard boxes she had unpacked. They grabbed what they thought was her handbag. Miss Day pretended to be unconscious until they left. All they took was the handbag she had been holding. As for the handbag it was one she was going to put on display."

"That was a clever move on her part I must see her now."

As I parted the screens I could see Grace, a welcoming sound entered my ears.

"Sorry peter I know you're busy but your chief insisted he send you, I didn't want to worry you, constable Arnold has left Sergeant Green at the shop so the workmen can carry on with my new kitchen."

"I really love you, where are you hurt and why the sling on your left arm?"

"No broken bones, just bruised, your boss Chief Jack Taylor said you could run me home, I would like to see the thieves faces when they saw the bag was full of packing paper."

"I will let Inspector Forward know as we are teamed up on a case."

Constable Arnold took Gracie's statement and left.

Once Grace was ready, carol drove us to the shop and helped me in with her, as she was still a bit unsteady.

Constable Arnold picked up Sergeant Green from the shop and left us there to settle Grace in but not until Carol had cooked her a breakfast. The workmen said they would keep an eye on Grace until they left at 5.30pm. I told Grace I would be back at 5.15pm before they left.

Carol had a call on her mobile as we crossed the road.

"Alistair Baker is awake and able to be interviewed. Let's get back to the hospital and see if we can get some answers.

Baker was sitting up in bed but was white as a sheet, his expression as we entered enter his room must have been the same as mine when I first set eyes on my ex mother in-law.

"Don't worry Mr. Baker we haven't come to take you back to your cell in fact Chief Inspector Stewart here is convinced of your innocence."

"I am innocent, I knew Thompson had been to her flat but as I lay in the hospital after my operation I could think more clearly. Thompson must have been pestering Kelly, if only I had believed her instead of thinking the worst she may still be alive today. "

"I am sure Thompson has framed you for Miss Hope's murder and I have worked out how he did it; Inspector Forward here is in charge of the case and has agreed to have an open mind."

"Thank you both for believing me but I understand my prints were on the gun, how on earth can I explain that?"

"Chief Inspector Stewart believes That Thompson put the gun in your hand while you were still unconscious in the recovery room."

"Some one would have noticed a member of the public in recovery, surly Inspector Forward?"

"Thompson is a porter at the hospital so would not be out of place."

"I really loved Kelly. Even though I thought she was seeing him I lived in hope it was just a temporary thing."

"I will leave you with Inspector Forward while I have a word with the doctor, about your chances of walking a return journey of six miles that day."

The doctor told me that at that stage the wound would have been inflamed and even walking up a flight of stairs would have been very painful as he has a secondary infection. I told Carol and we left to talk to the surgical staff, mainly to find out if Thompson was assigned to those duties that day. Apparently, it is who is available at the time. Thompson was at work that day but on general duties. "Another dead end Carol, look! That's the nurse Thompson was getting fresh with; let's have a word with her."

"Excuse us, I am Inspector Forward and this is Chief Inspector Stewart, we would like a word if your not to busy?"

"I know who you are, you rescued me from that creep Thompson, what did you want to know?"

"We need to know if you saw Thompson in the recovery room when Mr. Baker had his appendix out."

"I was in casualty that day but Clare Langridge was in charge of the recovery that day. Mr Baker would have been at theatre three, that's the one used for appendicitis. You will probably find her having her lunch break at this time, in the staff room at the end of this corridor on the left."

We entered the staff room, only to find it empty. A vending machine stood in the corner of the room calling out to my dry throat. Two hot chocolates were the order of the day. As we sat savouring every drop a nurse entered, I must admit she awakened the beast in me instantly, not just her slim shapely figure and sixties hair do but it was the way she had administered her make up and her dark mysterious eyes.

A sudden burst of pain in my calf snapped me out of the spell that had captivated my feelings. Carol sat glaring at me, her green-eyed face, staring angrily at me

I started to stand up in anticipation of talking to the nurse but as my knees started to lock Carol stood up; she put her hand on my shoulder and pushed me back down on my chair as she shook her head at me.

Carol walked over to the nurse and sat at her table, I could not hear the conversation as they were at the other end of the room.

Carol returned shortly looking puzzled.
"That is Clare Langridge, so if you put your eyeballs back in their sockets I will fill you in on our conversation."

"Sorry Carol but I am only human and it's normal to admire beauty, I am more than happy with Grace and I would never let her down."

"I still have feelings for you Peter and I still get jealous, anyway back to Clare Langridge, she claims that Thompson was working in casualty that day and never came near the recovery room."

"I don't understand how she would know that he was working in casualty and how come the last nurse we talked to was working in casualty, never mentioned seeing Thompson there."

"Your right Peter, they contradict each other so let's go to casualty and talk to some of the staff and try to get this straight."

The receptionist was sick on that day but that was a godsend. The staff remembered what happened on that day owing to the chaos her absence caused. No one even remembered seeing Thompson that day. Someone must be in charge of him, and we both wanted to know his movements.

"I've had enough of this Peter, I am going to have Thompson arrested until I get to the bottom of his movements."

"What will you have him arrested on? We don't have any evidence against him."

"Wasting police time and with holding evidence, anything! Until we get some answers from him."

Inspector Forward was true to her word, he was at the station within the hour. Because of my dislike for Thompson, Inspector Forward would not let me in the interview room, although I am her chief but I would never undermine her authority, it is her case. The result of the interview was damming to my theory. Apparently, he was helping the maintenance man in the staff quarters at the time of the shooting. If he were telling, the truth things would look bad for Alistair Baker.

"I think we should verify his story as soon possible Carol."

"You are right we should; do you still think Baker is innocent?"

"You're going by evidence, I'm going by gut feeling, how many people have been framed by false evidence and convicted?"

Carol asked reception to contact their maintenance man and have him report to reception for an interview. The man's name was Mr. Gary Hand. A few minutes later, a short grey haired man in a bib and brace appeared.

"Hello Mr. Hand this is chief Inspector Stewart and I am Inspector Forward, I would like to ask you about the 22nd of this month."

"That was the day the girl was murdered, I don't see how I can help."

"We understand you were working in the staff quarters that evening; perhaps you can tell us if you were working on your own and at what time."

"I started at 4.20pm and finished at 7.40pm; I had to re plum the kitchen due to damage to the pipe work; what has that got to do with the girl?"

"Did you have anyone help you do the work?"

"Trevor helped me move the fridge, freezer and cooker; he is a porter, his surname is Thompson, he can vouch for me."

"Was he with you the whole time, it's very important?"

"He came to give me a hand, must have been just after 4pm and apart from going to the fish and chip shop he was here till I finished."
"What time did he go to the chip shop? It could be vital to our enquiries."
"I can't be sure but we were both getting hungry; ah yes he said he normally had his bite to eat about 5pm; it must have been about 5.10pm when he left for the chip shop, he returned about 5.40pm with the fish and chips."
"Thank you Mr. Hand you have been very helpful, the chief and I will let you carry on with your duties, many thanks again."
I felt sorry for the old boy as he slowly walked away back down the corridor; he should have retired by now as he was clearly, worn out.
"Looks like your still in with a chance with your theory Peter."
Sister May Sellers was in her office, she seemed a nice person but very devoted to her job and not someone that would put up with any nonsense. She looked very smart in her uniform and little white hat, even though she was nearly 6ft tall and slightly stocky; trouble was she backed up Thompson's story as she saw him leave and return with the food. She did however say that someone had mentioned to her that one of the nurses was going out with one of the porters, apparently, there are five porters.
"I think we had better call it a day for now Peter, you have 35mins to get to Grace

before the workmen leave, so get those sexy hairy legs moving."

It was lucky Carol had reminded me of the time, as my head was so full of the case I had lost track of the time.

Carol gave me a peck on the cheek as she dropped me off at Gracie's, I felt relieved to arrive in time before the workmen left, that was until I spotted the police car outside. In panic mode, I rushed inside, only to find 2 youths sitting back to back on the floor bound together with masking tape.

"Hello Chief these workmen caught these two after Miss Day spotted them looking through the window, these are the two that grabbed the handbag."

"Thank you Constable Arnold; you gentlemen will get a bonus for capturing these two and looking after Miss Day. As for you two I think I will have a word with you in private."

"Sorry Chief I can't let you do that, I know what your temper is like."

"Ok Constable Arnold, perhaps one of these brave gentlemen will release them so you can cuff them, I will see if Inspector Saunders can come and give you a hand to get them back to the station."

"He has already gone home but Sergeant Green is at the station."

"Bulldozer is a good choice; Green didn't get that nickname for nothing."

Sergeant Green turned up and the two youths were taken into custody.

The workmen left leaving Gracie and I to settle down for the evening.

Although Grace was no longer at risk she insisted I stay with her for the night, to my surprise she had bought me a change of clothes and an electric shaver for me, she hopped to have me stay for the odd night.

I am not complaining but I felt a bit uneasy Grace was taking me for granted.

When I woke the next morning I felt I was on holiday, lying in a strange bed with a smile on my face. A lovely breakfast and a lovely smiling face looking at me over the table; it certainly set me up for the day ahead.

After breakfast, I telephoned Inspector Forward to pick me up.

As I was leaving, Grace asked if I would like to have dinner with her that evening, I smiled and nodded in agreement. Gracie's cooking was always delicious, how could I refuse to let her spoil me.

"Had a good night have you Peter?"

Carol asked as I opened the car door.

"Well it's time to get back to reality chief! I want to try and find out if Thompson was courting one of the nurses."

"Did you get the name of the nurse that slapped Thompson? She would probably know if he's courting."

"Yes; let's start with her; I think she would love to make trouble for him."

As Carol parked the car at the hospital, I spotted the nurse through the glass doors getting a drink from the vending machine.

By the time, we entered the hospital the nurse had disappeared and a doctor was at the vending machine. Carol asked him if he knew the name of the nurse who had just obtained a drink. We were in luck once Carol told him who we were he named her as Anna Young. Carol asked if she was courting, he told us that she was a bit of a loner and had just had a bust up with her fiancée but he did not know her fiancées name. Pointing to casualty, he told us we would find her there. We found her and another dead end, her fiancée worked at a betting shop in the town and the break up was over his excessive drinking. Asked if she knew whether Thompson was seeing anyone, she shrugged her shoulders. We decided to ask the receptionist but according to her, no one would touch him with a barge pole, mainly because of his crude manor.

Even with Thompson's alibi, I was sure he had had something to do with the murder and some how I would work out the part he played.

Back at the station, Carol and I decided to go over the statements Miss Hope's neighbours had made; in the hope that something would give us a lead.

Two hours and three coffees more I stumbled over a statement. Miss Trudy Trench in the flat above made, thought she heard a car backfire around 5.20pm, She was surprised it was so loud, her being on the seventh floor.

"Look at this Carol; why was this not brought to our attention?"

"You're right, she may have been shot earlier, but the time of murder was placed at 6pm, that was when some one else heard a gun shot."

"This statement is the only one that has mentioned a time they heard the gunshot, who took the statements?"

"I was busy so I sent constable Sky; would you like me to fetch her?"

"That would be a good idea and I have never been told who found the body."

"We had a phone call from someone claiming that they had heard a gunshot from Miss Hope's flat at 6pm. Green and Arnold accompanied me and broke in, I will fetch Constable Sky."

Although I was annoyed that vital clues had been overlooked, it did give me new hope. Carol soon returned with a sheepish looking Constable Brenda Sky.

"Sit down Constable Sky; we just need to ask you about the statements you took at the murder scene, for a start what questions did you ask the neighbours about the shooting?"

"I asked if they had heard a gun shot and some were not sure but about four others did hear a loud bang."

"Did you ask what time they heard the gun shot or loud noise?"

"No; we already new that she was shot at six o'clock by the phone call."

"Do you realise that you have wasted our time because of your assumptions? She was actually shot at 5.20pm; the phone call was probably made by the killer to mislead us and give them an alibi."

"I really am sorry; I just took it for granted the caller was telling the truth."

"Apologise to Inspector Forward, this is her case, I will leave you two together, it's up to Inspector Forward if she wants to discipline you."

As I left the room, I could hear Constable Sky burst into tears, followed by Carol telling her not to worry in a comforting voice.

All I could think of was Thompson's alibi has been shattered but still the only evidence was against Baker.

Constable Sky appeared a few minutes later still looking weepy and red eyed.

"Cheer up Miss Sky you look like my mother-in-law the day some one scratched her 250 Norton motor bike." she smiled and said.

"Thank you sir and I took your advice about my mascara; I now buy the same as you're Miss Day."

"Get yourself a Coffee and have a rest for a while, I will pop and see Inspector Forward; I think you will see it's all forgotten now."

I felt sorry for her as she walked away looking like a scolded little girl , she is a really lovely woman, she is a good all rounder, slim long blond hair, very pretty and her personality was also very attractive.

As I turned to return to the office, I was face to face with Carol.

"Did you have to upset Constable Sky? You know she gets upset easily."

"She is fine; we had a chat and I told her to get a coffee, have a break and all is forgotten, at least she will be on the ball next time she takes statements."

"How dare you leave me to reprimand her and then tell her every thing is ok?"

"Sorry but I knew you would let her off and she needed to know I was ok with it to, I won't interfere again, honest."

"I suppose you're over the moon Thompson is back in the running, you still can't prove any connection with him and the shooting."

Constable Sky returned with an envelope for Carol.

"No need to hand your resignation in to Inspector Forward Miss Sky." I said jokingly.

"It's from the coroner for Inspector Forward about the day I took those statements; I remember the flat opposite remarked about a postman often popped into Miss Hope's for coffee, but not the usual one."

"Thank you Constable we will look into it. Let me see what the coroner has to say, perhaps we may have some more to go on."

"There may have been three men in her life." Exclaimed inspector Forward.

"Guess what Peter; Miss Hope was three months pregnant and was already dead when she was shot; her neck was broken."

"The photos taken of the murder scene showed her sitting in the armchair. The one who shot her may have thought she was asleep. What are the chances of two separate killers turning up the same night?"

"Your right Peter; at least we know we are looking for a man."

"Don't be side tracked by the pregnancy; a jealous woman could be involved"

"I think I will get Sky and White to track down the postman while we get the reactions from Thompson and Baker about her pregnancy; unless you have a better plan Peter."

"It's your case and to be honest, that would have been my next move."

Baker broke down when we told him about the baby and he had been unaware of her pregnancy; he remarked some one had murdered his baby on the assumption he was the baby's father.

Thompson on the other hand referred to her as a tramp; he said they had never had intercourse and it was nothing to do with him. I could have decked him there and then.

Miss Hope in my mind was in love with Baker and he was the father, but she may have been involved with some one else, only tests could prove whether the baby was indeed Alistair Baker's.

It was 3.45pm when Constable Sky and Constable White returned to the office after following up on the bogus postal worker. They had obtained a description of the postie from Mr Tap, the neighbour who had observed the person visiting Miss Hope. The post office was positive no one of that description worked for them. I asked for a copy of the neighbour's description and statement. I then decided to accompany Carol to have a word with Mr Tap.

We found Mr Tap sitting in a wheel chair by the landing window reading a book, being in his fifties and on his own he lead a lonely life; he spent most afternoons on the landing and although being wheel chair bound he was very clean and tidy, as was his flat.

The normal postman always delivered the post around 10am and the visitor always arrived between 4pm and 5pm on different days of the week.

Mr Tap informed us, he was having tests at the hospital on the evening Miss Hope was murdered.

"I find it hard to tell some one's height sitting in my wheel chair, the person was the same height as this lady and always combed their hair before ringing Miss Hope's door bell, the comb had gem stones along the handle, I never saw the face"

"To recap Mr. Tap, the person is in your opinion approximately 5ft 10", wears the previous version of a postie, brown shoes, uses a comb studded by gem stones and calls on odd days in the week, after 4pm."

"That's correct, apart from the smell of aniseed and the wig, I only know that because the comb got snagged one day and I spotted it move."

"We could do with some one like you on the force Mr Tap; don't you agree Chief Inspector?"

"Yes Inspector Forward, perhaps you need another word with Sky and White."

"Point taken, thank you Mr. Tap, you have been invaluable to our investigations. Here is my phone number in case you remember anything else; by the way you haven't told us the colour of their hair."

"The wig was a light ginger and the glimpse I got when the wig moved was a mousey colour, good luck, my hospital appointment was at 5.15pm that evening. I hope you catch the one who murdered the poor girl, before my accident I was an Inspector in the force."

"That explains a few things, come on chief lets get back to the station."

On the way back to the station, Carol lost her temper with me because I suggested we check Thompson's work schedule, she was sick of me trying to pin the murder on him. I asked her to drop me off at my home, as I wanted to pick something up. Then I told her I would use my own car to make my own way back to the station, a white lie I know but although a good investigator she seems easily misled. The bogus postie, I felt sure was involved and as Thompson had light brown hair, made me think they were one of the same.

Instead of going to the station, I decided to return to the main sorting office and ask to speak to the oldest serving postal worker.

I waited in the manager's office and a few minutes later a grey haired man, named Fred Gorse entered. He had served on the post office for forty-two years and I felt he was a good bet to remember past or present employees. Apparently, he always left extra early for his rounds, this meant he only met a few of the staff. Unable to place anyone of that description he said.

"The one you want to talk to sir is Alice Burr. She has been here thirty-one years and although a really nice woman, is what you may call the local rag"

Alice Burr worked in the sorting office; this meant she was on site all day and new everyone's business.

Within two minutes, she had wormed out of me my engagement to Grace.

I stopped her in her tracks and gave her a description of the bogus postie.

"Five-ten, mousey hair, stinks of aniseed and uses a gem studded comb. The only one I can think of about that height and used a comb like that was Tony Strong but I don't remember the aniseed."

"Does he still work here? only he wore the previous type of uniform."

"Tony is a she. If she's the same person you're after, she left last summer. The early mornings seemed a problem for her, talk about lazy and could she pick them. She had so many black eyes we called her the Panda. She got the sack for her knack of causing arguments. She was finally fired on the spot when she threw a parcel at some one, which landed them in casualty for best part of the day."

"Any idea where she is now, or who her boyfriend was at the time?"

"I think she works at the hospital as a cleaner, as for her boyfriend he was jailed for robbing the milkman of his takings. His name is Harry Booker; he was always in trouble and always knocking Tony about."

After thanking Mrs Burr, I returned to the station to update inspector Forward. She finally agreed that the hospital was the common denominator, Baker had his operation at the same hospital Thompson and Strong work at, plus Strong may be the bogus postie. We set off to the hospital to try to find out.

When we arrived at the hospital, we requested to see Miss Strong. When she turned up, she was indeed about 5'10" tall with short mousey colour hair. As soon as Carol introduced us, Miss Strong shoved Carol out of the way and disappeared down the corridor. I helped Carol up and headed in the direction Strong had gone. We followed the exit signs on the assumption that she was trying to leave the hospital, reaching the exit at that part of the hospital and finding nothing we headed back towards the reception. We Were confronted by staff running towards us, seeing them disappearing into a ward we decided to follow, just in case Miss Strong was somehow involved.

The co-ordination and expertise of the doctor and nurses were very impressive, like a well-rehearsed play. A woman lay on the floor with blood oozing through her fingers as she gripped her chest.

"It's Miss Strong!" Carol shouted, looking confused. The nurse in charge of the ward claimed Strong had staggered hysterically into the ward before collapsing.

As the doctor tried to stop the bleeding, I asked her who her attacker was but before she could answer, two more doctors had turned up and lifted her onto a trolley. She glanced at the doctors and seemed to panic; she grabbed my arm and looked at one of the doctors. I noticed that he had a splatter of blood on one of his lapels on his white coat.

Her Panic at the sight of the doctor and the unexplained blood was enough for me to arrest him on suspicion of attempted murder. After removing his white coat for forensics to match the blood with Strong's, he was handcuffed by Carol as the emergency staff disappeared out of the ward with Miss Strong. The doctor suspected of the stabbing was Dr. Carl Wake; he certainly had a foul mouth as he pleaded his innocence.

Carol contacted Sergeant Green and Constable Arnold to take Mr. Wake into custody. We decided to wait and see if Miss Strong would pull through.

It was nearly an hour later when a surgeon appeared from the theatre.

"I take it you two are the police? we have done everything we can for Miss Strong. She has lost a lot of blood and the wound would indicate she was stabbed with a scalpel, she should make a full recovery."

"Why do you think it was a scalpel? No chance it could have been a screwdriver or something similar."

"The tip of a scalpel had snapped off in one of her ribs which saved her life; quarter of an inch either way and it would have punctured her heart"

Inspector Forward contacted Constable Arnold and told him to return to the hospital to protect Miss Strong. I was convinced my original theory was right, as the hospital seemed to be the common denominator. I spotted another porter about the same age as Thompson. After introducing myself, I asked if he was a friend of Thompson.

"Yes, we go for a drink and a game of darts sometimes, he is in the boiler room if you want him, you don't think Trevor had anything to do with Tony's stabbing do you? I know he has a vial temper but I can't see him doing that to her"

"We are just trying to find out about people as part of our investigations. Does he have a girlfriend, any family, any information at all?"

"He did go out with Tony for a while, that's Tony Strong, but she broke it off, he is always chatting up the nurses and did say he had come up trumps with one, he has a brother who lives on the outskirts of town"

"Thank you; at least we can update our information Mr.?"

"Gregg Grey; I'm just called G.G. by my friends; Trevor was over the moon when he finally made it with the nurse, but he seems to be a nervous wreck lately and has stopped talking to me about his private life"

"Perhaps we can get to the bottom of what is troubling him Mr. Grey, would you mind asking him to go to reception, we would like to have a word with him"

Mr. Grey nodded and disappeared through a service door. Carol and I made our way to reception to wait for Thompson to arrive.

"By the way Peter; have you been picking on your ex mother in-law again?"

"I haven't a clue what you're on about, I never speak to her"

"I still keep in touch with your ex and she told me her mother received a get well card from Dartmoor Prison, wishing her a swift return, as they missed her wrestling matches"

"What makes you think I sent it, you do have a suspicious mind?"

"Come off it Peter; what about the letter from immigration, giving her a month to leave the country, or she would be deported as an undesirable, what do you think she would do if she finds out it was you? No! I don't even want to think about the outcome."

"I think we have had this conversation before; I understand the manure they dumped on her front lawn still has swarms of flies covering it"

"I will tell her if you keep on; she reported it to sergeant Kemp on the front desk"

"Sid is a good sport; he will just shelf it; look! Here comes Thompson"

We took him to one side and asked the name of the nurse he is dating, which immediately brought an angry expression to his face.

"How dare you check up on me, it's none of your business who I go out with?"

"Everything is our business when it's a murder inquiry. It's a crime to withhold evidence and obstruct the course of justice, if you would rather be escorted to the station by chief Inspector Stewart it's up to you?"

"You two have been on my back ever since the shooting, I have seen Clare Langridge a few times but it's nothing serious, so is that it? Can I go now?"

"Yes; you can go for now while the chief and I speak to your girlfriend."

"Do you know who she is carol? The nurse who looks after the recovery room, the one you kept gawking at in the canteen."

"That's right; anyway she would have been missed if she had left her post"

When we arrived at the recovery room, Clare Langridge was waiting for the operation in progress to be completed. therefore, we grabbed the chance.

"Miss Langridge; you told me that Thompson was in casualty the evening of the 22nd but failed to tell us you were dating him"

"How did you find out? We kept it quite, you know how people gossip."

"Where were you when Tony Strong was stabbed?"

"Never heard of her and I wasn't aware anyone had been stabbed"

"Inspector Forward never mentioned Tony Strong was a woman; what have you got to hide? The ward Miss Strong collapsed in is only just down the corridor from here. I will go and get someone to relieve you and take you in for further questioning, Miss Langridge!"

Carol insisted I drove while she sat in the back with Miss Langridge, the green-eyed monster again, shame, I would have loved to swap places with Carol. We could not take chances with Miss Strong's life and leave Miss Langridge, a possible murderer loose in the hospital to try again.

The Foul-mouthed doctor Wake was insisting on a solicitor being present but when we pointed out we would have to officially charge him if he did and inform the hospital, he agreed to co-operate.

"I was walking up the corridor and as I turned the corner, that woman was running in my direction. She appeared to be running from theatre number three; she was holding her bloodstained chest. As she passed, she swung her hand at me, beckoning me out of the way, some of the blood from her hand landed on my white coat."

"You will have to stay here until we can verify your story, why didn't you tell inspector Forward all this at the time?"

"I am sorry; things have gone wrong for me lately; I shouldn't let my private life spill out on others. I believe you have a rather large policeman guarding her, can't you just tell him not to let me in her room if you think I'm a threat, I am really busy and we are short staffed."

"That would be the decision for Inspector Forward to make; she is in-charge of this case, what do you think Inspector Forward?"

"Even your mother in-law couldn't get past Constable Arnold; I guess that would be ok. Ask sergeant Green to run him back to the hospital but make sure constable Arnold is introduced to the doctor first before he leaves's the hospital"

Once Sergeant Green had left with the doctor, Carol asked Sergeant Reed to bring in Miss Langridge. First thing Carol asked her was what number theatre she worked in. It was no surprise to find out it was number three.

"Inspector Forward, we had better get back to the hospital as quickly as possible, I need to check something out."

Without question, Carol told sergeant Green to put Miss Langridge back in the cell and followed me back to the car.

Back at the hospital, I collared a nurse to take us to theatre three. I hoped to find a trace of Miss Strong's blood, mainly to ascertain where she was at the time she was attacked.

"You must be joking Peter, Langridge would have cleaned it up but it was worth a try." After a thorough search and finding nothing, we went back to the corridor, both deep in thought. We had to move to the left of the doors as a patient was being wheeled in, as the doors were pushed open something caught my eye. The doors swung shut as the crew disappeared through them. As I pushed the right door open, there on the inside edge was a bloodstained fingerprint.

"Phone forensics Carol and I will wait here to make sure no-one wipes it off."

My feelings were mixed, I was over the moon we had found a clue but on the other-hand I hated the thought of Miss Langridge being jailed for attempted murder, but there again someone like that is better locked up.

Time was getting on and I just wanted to get home and relax, put my feet up in front of the television and watch a good film. Carol agreed it had been a long day and after our forensics man Henry Waters had finished we headed off to our homes.

   I was very tired as I drove home. On the way I was sure I spotted Thompson cross a pelican crossing I had stopped at, he was wearing a suit and a trilby hat. Knowing I must have been mistaken, as he was still doing his late shift at the hospital I put it down to fatigue.

 I arrived home to find Grace had let herself in with the key I had had cut for her. She did not look very happy, so I asked what was up and tried to give her a hug.

"Don't hug me! Who is Helen? I checked your answerphone and some women left you a massage which said, **'Its Helen, I need you're help. Please phone me, I know you can sort things out.'-** well who is she?"

"The only Helen I know is my ex wife and I haven't spoken to her for months; why did you pry into my answer machine? I would never dream of snooping into your private business."

"I am sorry, what can I say? It won't happen again. Why don't you phone her and see what's so urgent?"

"You phone her. Her number is in the book under **G.R.** for good riddance. Tell her I am in the shower and ask what she wants."

"I can't phone her, she will wonder who I am, you phone her."

"You took the message it's down to you. As far as I am concerned, there never was a message. It's up to you."

She phoned Helen and she said someone was ridiculing her mother, pointing out that her mother was Peter's ex mother in-law. She needed Peter to find out who is behind it.

"Well, that's what she said Peter, what are you going to do about it?"

"I will put inspector Forward onto it. We aren't allowed to get personally involved in cases, especially with people that fly around on broom sticks."

"Don't be so horrible, I am sure she is a very nice woman."

"They even refused to have her in the horror section of Madam Tussaud's."

"Let's forget about your ex and have some dinner I cooked, I've brought a good film to watch as well, how about that?"

"Sounds good, if I fall asleep through the film just make me comfortable."

We had the dinner, which was delicious and Grace was so attentive towards me during the film. Yes, she stayed the night.

I thoroughly enjoyed waking up next to Grace and having breakfast together. Although the nurse, Miss Langridge, is very desirable, she could never come close to Grace. Something about Grace just made me tingle all over. As I sat at the table with my empty plate and mug in front of me admiring Grace someone frantically knocked at my front door, bringing me back to reality. After making sure my bathrobe was done up I opened the door. There stood Inspector Forward, out of breath and red in the face.

"What is up with you Carol? It's only 6am!"

"Sergeant Reed is in hospital and Miss Langridge has gone."

"I don't believe it! I will get some cloths on."

"Do you have to Peter? I like you better without."

"**Who is it Peter**? **Is everything ok?**" Grace called out.

Carol looked embarrassed and apologised in a very soft voice.

"**Its Inspector Forward Grace, Something has cropped up.** Come in Carol."

Grace made Carol a cup of tea while I got dressed and Carol updated her as to why she had turned up early.

On the way to the hospital, Carol filled me in on what had transpired. Sid Kemp on reception had gone to the cells to find sergeant Reed and found him slumped against a wall in the cell Miss Langridge had been put in. She must have slipped out of the station while sergeant Kemp was attending to him.

"How badly is Sergeant Reed hurt? She was searched for anything she could have used as a weapon."

"They think he has concussion, looks like he fell backwards and hit his head against the wall, Ted has a large bump on the back of his scull."

Shortly after we arrived at Ted Reed's bed a doctor entered the room.

"Your Sergeant Reed is a lucky man; he is in a stable condition and should recover with no lasting damage. It would appear that tea had been thrown in his face and luckily he must have closed his eyelids in time; thank goodness."

"What a bitch! Sorry. It makes me mad to think he was doing her a kindness and she did this to him."

"Calm down Sir; the doctor doesn't need to hear that sort of outburst."

The doctor smiled and said. "Don't worry, reminds me of home, I thought of something far worse to describe her, it must be horrific to have your eyesight taken from you."

The doctor checked Ted then left.

"What made Ted go to the cells in the first place?"

"Sid had made tea for himself, Ted and Miss Langridge; Ted took her tea to her and when Ted hadn't returned after ten minutes Sid went looking for him."

"She must have thrown the tea in his face, pushed him, he lost his balance and fell against the wall. I suppose that's better than a scalpel in the ribs."

"That's about the size of it Peter but wouldn't it be a good idea if Sergeant Kemp was always accompanied to the cells?"

"As far as I am aware Carol, at our station no cell holding a prisoner was allowed to be opened unless two officers were present."

"Just goes to show sir, never underestimate a woman."

"Perhaps he would like to see a pretty woman when he wakes up? contact constable Sky to come and sit with him and let us know when he comes to."

"I will, I already have every available officer looking for Miss Langridge, I have sent Sergeant Green to bring Thompson back in to custody, he does seem to be deeply involved with this case."

Thompson refused to talk and Miss Langridge was still at large when Baker appeared in court for murder. As the trial progressed, all the jury were concerned with was the evidence. The blazing row Baker had had with Miss Hope and the motive being jealousy, I could see the jury all nod when the prosecution pointed out that his finger prints were on the murder weapon. I nudged Carol as I observed a woman in the jury take two silver tubes out of her handbag and hold them up in front of her.

"What's she doing Carol?"

"She is seeing which lipstick she wants."

"But they look identical how would she know without opening them?"

"You wouldn't unless you look at the base."

"I need to talk to the defence and get the court adjourned until tomorrow, I think I have worked it out, come on lets see her."

Mrs Trudy Sturgeon defending Baker told the judge that new vital evidence has been brought to her attention, for which She asked for a postponement and he agreed to postpone the proceedings until the following afternoon.

First call was to forensics and to look at the report they had done on the gun. Henry Waters in charge of forensics showed me the plastic bag containing the murder weapon and a separate bag containing the remaining bullets.

"There is no mention in the report about finger prints on the bullets Mr Waters."

"But there was no need the gun was covered in prints."
"You had better check them now and be quick about it; call yourself an expert?"
Waters went red in the face and Carol gave me the thumps up and smiled.
We waited while he checked the bullets for prints then he declared.
"One thing is certain it wasn't Baker that loaded the gun, I really am sorry I should have checked everything. By the way the coroner Mr Watson is pretty sure she was killed within half an hour before being shot."
"Give me a report to that affect."
I telephoned Colonel Samson to ask is the gun was loaded when it was stolen. The gun was not loaded but a new box of bullets is missing. This was in our favour; we just had to match the fingerprints on the bullets.
Carol and I set off to the hospital to see if my next theory was correct."
      At the hospital, I asked the I.T. man to show me the footage taken of the front entrance the night of the shooting. It clearly showed Thomson leave then return with the fish and chips.
"That was a waist of time sir we already know all this, it proves nothing."
"Come on lets see if I am right, we have two more calls to make."
      We arrived at the fish and chip shop and as I had already observed when I checked out Thompson's alibi there was a C.C.T. camera.

47

"Hello Dave; did you keep the footage I told you to? I would like Inspector Forward to see it."

He took us to his office and showed us the footage of him serving Thompson.

"What can you see Inspector Forward? Anything that jumps out at you."

"Not really sir, it's in black and white, all you're doing is proving Thompson's innocence."

"Think, remember the footage at the hospital, and now compare it with this."

She watched it, then, rewound it again, then, she smiled.

"It's a different shirt; the lapels of the collar button up on this one and look as he is leaving you can see he has double vents on the back of his jacket, as he left the hospital it was a single vent; I don't understand. It certainly looks like him."

"The other night on the way home I thought I was seeing things, till I found out Thompson's brother is an identical twin. The maintenance man Mr Arnold told me the pipe work he had to repair had been deliberately vandalised. Thompson knew Mr Hand would need help with the kitchen and that would give him an alibi, his brother doubled for him at the chip shop while he went to Miss Hope's flat and murdered her by breaking her neck.

Miss Langridge had pressed Bakers hand on the gun in recovery the week before to incriminate him and cover her tracks. I checked with the surgeon who said no operation was scheduled the evening of the 22nd so Miss Langridge had plenty of time to get to and from the flat from the hospital; I don't know what the motive would be or what part Miss Strong played in it."

"We need to have another talk to Mrs Lewis at flat 5, it's just a hunch."

We arrived at flat five and Mrs Lewis apologised for being in her dressing gown and curlers but offered us a cup of tea, in fact she insisted.

"Sorry to bother you again but could you think back to the evening Miss Hope was shot and tell us if you noticed anyone at all enter the building around 5pm?"

"There were no callers only the paramedic, but I think it was a false alarm."

"Why do you think it was a false alarm and could you describe the paramedic?"

"It was only a female paramedic; she was only in the building about five minutes then left again in one of those estate cars they use."

"Looks like I got things back to front, Thompson must have pulled the trigger."

"Thank you Mrs Lewis I will be sending you a little gift, we're very grateful."

"Thank goodness that lady juror decided to retouch her lipstick, the fact they looked like bullets made you think of the prints and as they looked identical made you think of his twin brother. You have a good mind but no motive."

"You have Thompson locked up so lets have a word with him."

After telling him that we had proof of his guilt concerning Miss Hope's murder he went pale in the face; he sat wringing his hands for a while.

"I will tell you everything I know, I really fancied Miss Hope so I popped round to her flat a few times, she said she wasn't interested as she was in love with that blasted Baker bloke. I turned up there on one occasion with a couple of cream cakes, one I had drugged and had sex with her. She never reported me because she thought she would lose her precious Baker but when she realised she was pregnant started to blackmail me into stealing drugs for her."

"The chief and I would like to know where Miss Strong fits into all this."

"She was the one Kelly used to pick up the drugs from me at the hospital, they had been friends for quite some time."

"How could you shoot a woman carrying your unborn child?"

"I never shot her; she was dead when I got there about 5.30pm; I used the back entrance so that nosey old woman on the 1st floor couldn't see me; I went there to tell Kelly one of the staff had found out and there would be no more drugs."

I handed him a plastic wallet I had put my wristwatch in on the way to the cells after wiping my prints off. I asked him to remove and examine the watch and asked if he recognised it, he shook his head and replaced it in the bag.

"Come outside Inspector Forward and lock the cell door. I want to check something; I will be back in a moment."

Yes, I went straight to Henry Waters to compare his prints with the ones on the bullets. I was shocked when he shook his head. I returned to the cell Carol was waiting outside and told her.

"Well Peter, all we can charge him with at the moment is rape and theft of drugs. That's your theory out of the window."

"I suppose we had better compare Baker's prints before proceeding any further."

Baker's prints did not match either so everything pointed to Miss Langridge.

On the way to our offices, we had a call from Constable Arnold who was guarding Miss Stone. A nurse had wanted to see her to give her some medicine but he took it from the nurse and refused her entry to the room. We returned to the hospital and took the medicine to the hospital lab for analysis in case of foul play. I cannot pronounce the name of the drug but it would have had the same effect of taking 65 sleeping tablets in one go. We returned to constable Arnold and praised him up for saving Miss Strong's life. I would certainly put a recommendation in to chief of police Jack Taylor.

The description of the nurse fitted Miss Langridge; no wonder no one could find her she had been hiding in the hospital. This was a perfect place to hide a nurse.

As we were talking, a nurse approached and told us some one had pressed the emergency bell in that room. We entered while Constable Arnold kept the nurse outside. Miss Strong had pressed the bell as she had come to and was in pain and very emotional; we sent the nurse to bring the sister in charge along with some painkillers. Carol asked Miss Strong what had led up to her attack.

"I had gone to theatre three to tell Miss Langridge that the police were asking questions. As I entered the recovery room, Miss Langridge was talking to Dr Wake. The doctor left the recovery room so I told her about us stealing drugs and the police were asking questions, she asked if I knew who the Dr was that was involved, I told her I did not know and left the recovery room.

Dr Wake was just outside as I left he thrust something into my chest. I pushed him away with both hands and as I put my hand on my chest it felt wet, my hand was covered in blood, I nearly fell backwards but grabbed the door frame.

I pulled myself forward and saw Dr Wake getting up off the floor, that's when I panicked and ran to the nearest ward."

"Stay beside her bed Constable and only let the sister attend to her."

Carol and I went looking for the murdering duo after asking the woman on reception to let us know if she spots either of them. After rushing in and out of rooms and up and down corridors for a while, we decided to call in a team of officers to help. A nurse rushed up to us and told us our constable needed us urgently. As we entered Miss Strong's room, Constable Arnold standing over the sister lying face down on the floor confronted us.

"What have you done?" Carol shouted. "It's the sister."

He shook his head as he turned her over with his size twelve boot.

There lay Miss Langridge complete with the sister's uniform and hat, out cold.

"Have you killed her constable? Peter! you had better check on the real sister."

As I left the room, a woman in a petticoat came running towards me.

"Chief Inspector Nurse Langridge attacked me, she has my uniform."

"I'm afraid my constable has hit her and she is unconscious in Miss Strong's room, perhaps you can take a look at her."

I smiled as I watched the sister examine her then start to retrieve her uniform.

My smile soon disappeared as Carols shoe skimmed across my shin.

"You are an old prude Inspector Forward; do you need a hand sister?"

"Yes can you sit her up so I can pull her arms out the sleeves?"

As I sat her up Carol stormed out the room, the sister soon had her uniform back on, leaving Miss Langridge on the floor in just bra and briefs. I took a blanket off the bed, after covering her with it and with the help of Constable Arnold put her on the bed. The sister fetched Langridge's clothes from her office and dressed her. As the sister had just finished dressing her she came to. Carol came back, helped to dress her, and soon had the handcuffs on.

Sergeant Green turned up to guard Miss Hope while Constable Arnold finished his shift and went home.

Carol and I took Miss Langridge to the station to try to find out the motives these nasty low lives had.

After a long spell of silence we charged her with murder and attempted murder, she decided to make a statement.

According to Nurse Langridge She had known Miss Hope since her school days and kept in touch, she was aware that Thompson had seduced Miss Hope after drugging her and that he was supplying her with drugs from the hospital.

Miss Hope had stumbled onto something concerning some one at the hospital running a large drugs fraud. Thompson had picked up and given Miss Hope the wrong box containing instructions and a contact. He was supplying her with morphine as she suffered with bad migraines and damage to her neck due to whiplash.

Earlier on that day of the murder, she had a call from Miss Hope telling her what she had found, all she had said was that a Dr in the hospital was running it and she would make a copy of the letter to give to her. This was the first time she was aware of what was going on and decided to keep quite until she found out, who the Dr was so she could put a stop to it.

"Did you see her that day; a female paramedic was seen there about 5pm?"

"No I was helping out in theatre one because our theatre three hadn't any operations scheduled that afternoon."

"Did Miss Hope ever mention that someone often visited her in the afternoons wearing a postie's uniform and a ginger wig?"

"She never had visitors except her boyfriend Alistair then Thompson followed her from the hospital after Alistair's operation; I popped in the odd Sunday mornings to keep in touch."

"Why did you try to kill Miss Strong and pose as the sister?"

"I only put a sleeper hold on the sister so I could get past your police man guarding her because I was sure she was somehow involved; as for the medicine it was given to me for Miss Strong by Dr Wake before I posed as the sister. I was unaware of the contents I never gave it a thought."

"You will have to stay here while Inspector Forward and I try to find out who the Paramedic was that called at 5pm."

We managed to find out the name of the female Paramedic, Mrs June Tate.

We located her, she told us she had to call to a Mr. Tap on the sixth floor but when she got there, it was a false alarm, so left almost immediately.

"That's strange Peter Mrs Lewis at flat five never mentioned this bogus postie, I would have thought they would have stuck out like a monk at a strip club."

"You must have read my mind, in fact that's been puzzling me for a while, and I knew something was wrong but couldn't put my finger on it."

"The day is fast disappearing Peter and we only have the morning to find out who did kill her. let's get back to the station and run background checks on the people we have interviewed, it may give us a clue with any luck."

"That is certainly your forte Carol lets see you in action."

With that, she grabbed hold of me and started giving me a long lingering kiss.

"Not that sort of action! Anymore of that and I will have you arrested for sexually assaulting a police officer, do I make my self clear?"

"What an old grouse you've become chief Inspector Peter Stewart, get your sorry backside back to the car and let's go and start investigating."

I gave her a peck on the cheek, pinched her bum a told her we were even, she smiled and skipped back to the car looking like a cheeky chimp.

After a coffee and sandwich, Carol started her magic on the computer checking out first the Dr Carl Wake. He had never been married, no brothers or sisters and no criminal record. Next, was Miss Clare Langridge, one brother living in Scotland and her parents living in London but no criminal record? Mr. Trevor Thompson we had already checked him out, he did had a record, and twin brother. Miss Tony Strong had no criminal record and no living parents, just a sister that nothing is known about and unable to trace. Without thinking, Carol typed in Mrs June Tate, to our surprise, her maiden name was Tap. Carol researched further and uncovered Mrs Tate was Mr Tap's daughter. We looked at each other and both came to the same conclusion. Mr. Tap tried to incriminate Strong with the bogus postie story thinking it would confuse the case, it certainly wasted a lot of time.

"Mrs Tate must have brought her father the gun at 5pm and if you are thinking the same as I am, Tap had already killed Miss Hope but shot her at 5.20pm to put the blame on Baker. One of them knew Colonel Sampson was in hospital and robbed his house gun and all, I wonder how many other patients they have robbed, a perfect setup, they have all the patients details and if they live alone.

Mr. Tap, Mrs. Tate and Dr Wake; were arrested and charged. Mr. Tap was convicted of 1st degree murder. It was his prints on the bullets and of peddling stolen drugs. His daughter Mrs Tate was charged with the attempted murder of Miss Stone and peddling stolen drugs. We found out she was the one posing as the nurse who brought the lethal medicine that Constable Arnold intercepted. Dr Wake was charged with stealing and supplying drugs and two counts of attempted murder. Stabbing Miss Stone and trying to poison her. Miss Strong was charged with aiding Thompson to steal drugs and Thompson was charged with stealing drugs and rape.

Nurse Clare Langridge was cleared of any charges. Miss Hope had told her, she was going to name her baby Chance as that would cover either sex and seemed appropriate. Nurse Langridge bought a nice headstone for Miss Strong. The first part of the inscription read.

Miss Kelly Hope and baby Chance together for always dearly missed.

Nurse Langridge became a good friend of Constable Arnold and they ended up courting. We all wondered if it would turn him from a rock into a big softie.

Together, Carol and I had proved we are a good team on the force and still felt there was something special between us. Although I had not predicted the correct outcome, evidence can cloud the truth. I still go by my gut feelings.

The obvious; is not always the **truth**

Be back soon

Chief inspector Peter Stewart

JAMES M DYET

PETER STEWART'S MURDER CASE'S

THE ELUSIVE
VIGILANTE

CASE 4

THE ELUSIVE VIGILANTE

Day 1

To my embarrassment, I was actually present when this murder took place.

My fiancée Grace had decided to take me with her to buy items for her new kitchen. As we were browsing in a department store, a loud crashing sound echoed from behind us. A smartly dressed man lay on the floor surrounded by pots and pans he had fallen against that had been on a display, I was first to reach the man, his eyes and mouth were wide open. He was stone dead but looked to have had a heart attack.

A man pushed me to one side declaring he knew first aid. I pulled him away before he could try to resuscitate the man. Having seen poisoned victims before I knew that might be how he had died. Glancing round the store, I could only spot one shop assistant, the first aid chap, a woman and small boy in a pushchair, plus two middle-aged women. I told them not to leave the area and put them all to the end of the section away from the exit.

After phoning the police station, I started taking names and addresses with their statements. Grace kindly took notes while I asked the questions but no one admitted seeing the man until he fell against the display.

To make sure they had given me the correct names etc, I checked their driving licences bank cards, anything they had just to verify their identities.

Simon Watson our coroner arrived with Inspector Carol Forward, Carol took all the details from Grace while Simon inspected the body.

"You are right Peter he has been poisoned and by the look of his face a rather fast acting painful poison."

"He was the other side of the isle when I heard him fall against the display, as the isle displays are only 5ft tall I would have seen someone run away. All the people in here at the time are over 5ft 6ins tall."

"What about the CCT camera's? Perhaps they recorded the incident Peter." Asked Grace.

"I will check that and by the way I recognise the victim, it's Derek Harper a nasty bit of work. He was a money lender and the people with a motive to kill him would fill a book."

"Sounds like you have your work cut out for you with this one? I think Inspector Forward is trying to attract your attention, Peter."

Carol just wanted to know if she could release the customers, as she and Grace had completed the statements. I gave the ok and took Grace and Carol to the main office, hoping to see the CCT footage of the incident.

The manager Mr. Page was extremely upset, thinking this would somehow affect his job, I told him I would send an impressive report to his bosses stating how efficient and professional he had been.

The footage showed the victim on his own in that isle and the other customer's one or two isles away. The shop assistant was talking to the two middle aged women. As no one was near the man when he fell, all I could do was, wait for the coroner to finish his autopsy.

This was supposed to be my day off with Grace so I thought I would ask Carol to look after things until tomorrow. She jumped at the chance and reminded me as she grinned; I owed her a favour. Leaving Carol and Simon the coroner at the scene, I took Grace out for a meal.

We decided not to buy anything for the kitchen that day as it would remind Grace of the murder. We picked some things up from my place for an overnight stay at Gracie's flat. When we arrived at Gracie's shop Simon Watson was waiting at the shop door. As we walked towards him, I could see he was concerned about something.

"Hello Simon, what brings you here? Would you like to come in for a coffee?"

"That would be a good idea, I will explain about the murder when we are inside."

We settled down with our coffees and waited to hear what Simon had to say.

"We were both wrong about the victim being poisoned; as we were putting him on the mortuary slab I had my left hand supporting his neck and my right on the back of his head. As I moved my hand away, something caught my hand.

A thin metal shaft had been projected through the base of the scull into his brain."

"I suppose his thick shoulder length hair must have hidden it and as it hadn't gone past the outer layer of skin, plugged the flow of blood."

"That's correct but the bit I am concerned about is the angle of projection."

"What do you mean? Surly it was fired from behind."

"Yes but at a 45% angle and must have been fired from about 3-4ft from the ground."

"I knew something was wrong but I never followed my gut feeling up."

"What on earth are you talking about Peter? Who are you talking about?"

"The kid in the pushchair, I never saw its face it was hooded but its fingers were fat, like an adults."

"You think it was a Dwarf? I suppose that would make sense, we have the woman's face on the CCT footage so that's a start."

Grace tapped me on my shoulder and said.

"I remember from the footage, the man glanced down to his left briefly just before he fell against the display."

"Looks like your theory about the assailant being a dwarf is correct Peter and as you hadn't heard a weapon going off it had to be a small type of crossbow."

"If you see Inspector Forward before I do, fill her in and ask her to get a copy of the footage so we can identify the woman."

Simon left and I made some notes for the morning, Grace and I thought we would practice our honeymoon by me carrying her over the threshold of the bedroom.

Day 2

   After a lovely breakfast, I left for work with a big smile on my face, that was until I reached the station and was told the chief wanted me urgently.

   A man called John Budd had been murdered in the early hours of the morning. He was a very violent man, although wanted for a string of crimes we could never make them stick. Inspector Forward was already on the scene, which was at 'The Happy Gambler Club'. According to the manager, an old woman had called at the main door to see Budd urgently, the manager saw Budd heading for the hall and later found him dead in the front lobby.

The paramedics that attended phoned the police owing to a metal shaft protruding from his chest. "That is the same type of bolt as the one that killed Derek Harper yesterday Carol. I see Simon has just arrived, bet he never expected another crossbow killing, in fact I bet he never had to do an autopsy on one before."

 "Hello Peter, Hello Inspector Forward, That's a crossbow bolt in his chest, not that mad dwarf again?"

"Why can't you call me Carol Simon? And no, it was an old woman according to the manager of the club."

"Sorry Carol, I think you two have got a couple of vigilantes on your hands."

"Either that or a tit for tat killing as they were rivals, what do you think peter?"

"I would bet on a vigilante, I don't think the same weapon would be used for a tit for tat killing, let's talk to the manager Carol and leave Simon to do his bit."

We found the manager Mr Jake Tate in his office nursing a hangover.

"We need to ask you some questions Mr Tate, I am chief Inspector Stewart and this is Inspector Forward."

"I've already told one of your constables what happened."

"What we want is a detailed description of the old woman, anything that struck you odd about her."

"I'm not very good at languages but she had a foreign accent and looked a bit like a gypsy. You can judge for yourself, it would be on the tape, there is a CCT camera recording anyone entering or leaving the club, just for security."

"We only caught a glimpse of the woman's face, when she turned her head while waiting for her victim to arrive. It was defiantly the same woman, she had a different wig but her Roman nose was unmistakable.

As John Budd approached the woman, she lifted a small crossbow from under her coat, then without speaking fired the bolt straight into his heart and calmly walked out of the door. Armed with the tape we left for the police station, all we knew was she was foreign, had a Roman nose and a dwarf as an accomplice.

Our chief Jack Taylor had Carol and I in the office to try to find a way of trapping the killers. Unable to come up with a positive plan we left. Within two days there have been two murders and like all murder cases your mind works overtime, searching for clues, as I lay in bed that night mine was burning its self out. 3am found me sitting in the kitchen drinking a cup of camomile tea to try to relax. My mind kept wondering on to gypsies, circus people and fairs, my gut feeling just kept disagreeing. By 3.45am, my head was spinning so much I went back to bed and fell into a deep sleep.

Day 3

My alarm clock woke me at 6am as usual and to my surprise I felt wide-awake and eager to face the task ahead. While having my breakfast the thought occurred to me all I had to do was phone all the doctors surgeries and ask if they have any dwarfs on their records. Inspector Forward would be the obvious choice for the job.

As soon as I arrived at the station, I had a word with Carol, she thought it was a brilliant idea and headed for her desk. Inspector Joe Roberts was also assigned to the case as he had been working on an armed robbery involving John Budd, the second victim. Joe had also been investigating Derek Harper on extortion charges, along with complaints of running a protection racket.

Joe came over and said. "Hello Peter, I haven't found any connection between the two victims, except they were both crooks. I wondered if it might be someone trying to take over their racket but there's nothing on the grapevine."

"I think they just picked on the wrong people, if that's the case the killers would have been victims in both men's rackets."

"I overheard you tell Carol to try and track the dwarf through the doctors, I think I will try that in the future if I get someone out of the ordinary."

"Just thought it was worth a try Joe, Carol will keep trying other avenues if that fails, I think we will have to call her the bloodhound, she won't give up and always seems to be hot on the crooks heals. If you can find out their normal haunts as the killers must have been following the victims for weeks, they knew exactly where they would be to carry out two murders in two days."

I went to our chief Jack Taylor to update him on our progress, which was zilch, although he was pleased at the avenues we were taking.

My frustration brought back my craving for chocolate again, if I had not become a tea total I would have been heading for the whisky about now. I realise now how the whisky dulled my sense of deduction and chocolate seemed to enhance it. As I reached the office door a hand landed on my shoulder, a voice said.

"Off to get some chocolate?"

I turned to see Carol grinning at me.

"How did you know what I was thinking Carol?"

"Every time you get stressed you squeeze the top of your nose between your thumb and finger then close your eyes for about half a minute."

"Not always, I often do that to think, but the craving doesn't always follow."

"Your right, but when you do it with your left hand you always get chocolate."

"Your observation skills are second to none, let me buy you a nice big bar and then see if you can use your skills to spot the killers."

As I was half way through my bar, Carol was already screwing her wrapper up. How she keeps, her lovely figure eludes me, unless she burns up her calories through mental overdrive.

I could not figure out how the killers knew Derek Harper would be at the super store so we drove to the Lucky Gamblers Club. On the other side of the road was a bank, jewellers and pawnbrokers. All had CCTV, which I hoped would over the few days before John Budd's murder, may show who followed him.

The Bank had the best view of the road and of the club so that was our first choice.

The Manager was only to glad to help find the killer as Mr. Budd had been a very good customer, mainly because he frequently deposited (large sums of money). I pointed out to him that the money was taken; violently from decent folk. The two days before he was murdered the CCTV footage showed that he visited the club always the same time of the day. The footage clearly showed the cloaked figure approach the main door of the club a few minutes after John Budd. Being cloaked we never got a glimpse of the person. We did however notice the same woman walk past the club just after Budd had entered. The day before the murder, she was pushing a pushchair.

"That's got to be them Peter, they must have gone there after killing Harper that's why she has the kid with her and sorry I mean the dwarf."

"That seems a safe bet so we will take the tape back to the office so we can study it properly."

The jeweller's camera just caught a glimpse of the woman but very briefly. We went to the pawnbrokers and to our delight; the camera gave us a full frontal of the woman and to our dismay a young boy of about 3-4yrs, old looking in the window of the shop.

"She is a really pretty woman and hasn't a roman nose, the boy has his hand on the window and his fingers look normal."

"The cloak looks the same as the killers Peter, but the footage being black and white it could be a different colour, I'm stupid, I haven't checked the address the woman with the boy or dwarf given to me at the department store."

"I'm sure that's not the same woman at the store, I would have remembered."

"You would, especially an attractive woman like that, men you're all the same."

"What's up with all this jealously? My life would be a living hell married to you. I'm with Grace and she has never shown any jealousy and she trusts me."

Carol stormed out of the shop and sat in the car. I took the tape and never had a word from her all the way back to the station.

After getting ourselves a coffee and sandwich from the vending machine, we retired to the conference room to study the tapes.

We watched the tape, which clearly showed a caped figure with a pushchair pass the club, minutes after John Budd entered the club, on the other side of the road. About 4mins after a caped figure with a pushchair passed the bank on this side of the road. The footage from the bank never gave us a look at the faces.

I decided to get our hot shot CCTV man in to see if he could zoom in on the figures. Carol returned with Terry Carter who gets a kick out of showing off his skills. He connected his laptop to the player and started to zoom in. Straightaway we noticed the wheels on the pushchair were of a different design second was the woman's shoes were different.

Carol shook her head and said.

"How often do you see two cloaked women on the same street? It's too much of a coincident."

Terry laughed. "You're out of touch Inspector Forward, every one's wearing them; they are selling like hot cakes at the market."

"Thanks Terry, I'm sure the woman in the department store did not have a Roman nose Carol, so there may be more than two involved."

"I'm sure your right, all we can assume from these tapes is they do their homework on their victims."

The chief Jack Taylor suddenly burst into the room, red in the face and out of breath.

"I want to see you two in my office, now!"

We left Terry to take care of the tapes while we tried to catch up with Jack.

We arrived at his office, he stood staring out of his window and said nothing for a few seconds, when he turned to face us he looked terrified and confused. He slumped in his chair and said in a defeated tone. "They kidnapped her."

"Who's been kidnapped? Is it someone you know?" I asked.

"My daughter I had a telephone call a few minutes ago telling me to drop the investigation into the thug's killings or risk losing my daughter."

I nearly said without thinking swap her with your mother-in-law but just stopped myself in time.

"They know you can't even if you wanted to chief."

"What am I going to do? I wish I had never taken the promotion to chief."

We all stood in silence for a while then I asked. "Have you phoned your daughter to see if she is missing?"

"I phoned my son-in-law, he said she went to the shop for some milk and hasn't returned, that was over an hour ago and the shop is in the next street."

"Come on Chief Inspector Stewart, we can start at the Chief's daughter's home and try to find some sort of clue."

"Ok Carol, we will keep in touch and let you know as soon as we find out anything Chief, my gut feeling tells me she has been misplaced not kidnapped."

When we arrived at his daughter's, his son-in-law Eric Lamb was sitting on his front door step clutching his cordless phone in his hand. He shook his head and said in a defeated voice.

"I tried her mobile, Jack said she's been kidnapped by some killers, please get her back I feel so helpless."

"Inspector Forward and I will certainly do everything we can and a photo of Ruth would help." He left and came back with a recent photo. "The chief and I need to know what she was wearing when she left."

"She had a white blouse and pearl necklace, beige pleated skirt, brown leather shoes and handbag to match."

Armed with the photo and description we headed for the shop.

Allan Tarrant owned the local shop, when we asked if Mrs Lamb had been in the shop that morning, he handed me a piece of paper and said.

"Ruth came in the shop just over an hour ago; she asked for some milk and asked if her magazine was in. I went to the back room to fetch it and as I re-entered the shop a woman was holding up Mrs Lamb and helping her towards the door. Mrs Lamb never spoke and looked, groggy, the woman helping her towards the door said.

"I take Mrs Lamb home, you not worry, I see her home."

"I had never seen the woman before so I followed them outside and I wrote the number plate on the paper your holding. The car was a black top, red BMW. She knew Mrs Lamb's name but it's been playing on my mind, I was just shutting up shop to take the milk and magazine to her, to see if things were ok when you arrived."

"Mrs Lamb has gone missing; Inspector Forward and I will put a trace on the car. Thank you for help and we will take the shopping to Mr Lamb and let him know what's happened."

"Tell Eric if there is anything I can do let me know. By the way the woman spoke in a foreign accent and her nose seemed a different shape."

"We thought it was the same woman we have been after, thanks Mr Tarrant."

As we pulled up outside Mr Lamb's house, I pointed up the road.

"Your right Peter, it's the car Mr Tarrant saw drive away with Mrs Lamb."

The car was parked about 150yds up the road. As we got near, we could see there was one occupant in the passenger front seat. It was Mrs Lamb and she appeared to be asleep. The car was unlocked and Mrs Lamb was just groggy and seemed unharmed. Carol and I helped her back down the road to her house.

Mr Lamb rushed out the front door and picked her up he cradled her in his arms as he took her indoors. He was very emotional as Mrs Lamb started to get her senses back. Carol was straight on the phone to Jack Taylor to give him the good news. Inspector Roberts answered the phone and said the chief was on his way to his daughters. As Carol put the receiver down a car screeched to a halt outside. Jack rushed up to the house still unaware that his daughter was home safe. I opened the front door and told him she was in the front room, his eyes started to fill and he smiled and nodded, then joined his son in-law with his daughter. Carol and I decided to go to the kitchen and get the kettle on.

A cup of tea seems to be an automatic reaction in troubled times. Why? I have never figured it out, still it seems to give comfort so why not.

After Ruth had shaken off her drowsiness, she told us the woman sprayed something in her face then everything was a blur, until we helped her out of the car.

"Your gut feeling was right Peter; you knew they weren't going to keep her."

"These are clever people and they know that your hands are tied, they wanted to prove a point, which was only the crooks are the ones they were after. I know you chief and if they had known you better, what they have done will be their downfall. I think it will be a good idea if you pretend to take a couple of weeks off but operate from home, give them a false sense of security."

"I'm full of rage at the moment but your right I will do as you suggest; I think I will spend the rest of the day here. I can't face the team at the yard at the moment."

When Carol and I arrived back at the station, the forensics team were just leaving to check the BMW out for prints etc. The car as we expected, had been stolen early that morning. The car was stolen from a car dealer's forecourt, so we thought we would see if any footage had been recorded of the car being stolen. The owner a Mr Donald Sawyer is suspected of selling cars after he had wound back the milometer, also given stolen cars a false identity.

As we entered his office, he was in his chair with his back to us and never responded to us. Carol looked at me and said.

"They must have killed him, you check him out please."

I walked to the front of him but couldn't see a bolt sticking out of him. I felt his neck for a pulse and told Carol to phone for an ambulance.

"The paramedic in charge was Andy Page. He had attended the Cheviot's at Woodland Grange. He said it appeared that Mr Sawyer was drugged. He tipped the remainder of his half-drunk coffee into a container and called his college, Steven Bates to bring a stretcher.

Carol phoned Constable Arnold to meet the ambulance at the hospital and guard Mr Sawyer in case the vigilante tried to finish him off.

As the ambulance drove away we locked up and walked back to the car.

"What's wrong Peter? You look troubled."

Carol asked as we put our seat belts on and waited for an answer before turning the ignition on.

"Why Jack Taylor's daughter? They are not as clever as I thought they were. Jack must know who they are, even though he doesn't realise it."

"I see what you mean, perhaps the chief will remember before they kill again."

"Perhaps they are going to make sure he doesn't, that may be why they changed their mind about kidnapping his daughter. Send Sergeant Green round to his daughter's and stay with the chief until we can find somewhere safe for him."

When we arrived at the station Carol pulled all the case's the chief had worked on, she looked excited thinking of how she would solve the case. I took Carol a black coffee and a cheese sandwich then left for the hospital.

Nothing added up, Mr Sawyer had arrived at his car sales to find the car gone so how did the drugs get in his coffee. These people do not mess about with drugs they just kill instantly.

Constable Arnold said that, Mr Sawyer was not likely to regain consciousness until the morning. I decided to return to his office and check the CCTV coverage of that morning.

The woman with the Roman nose was on the film stealing the BMW. About an hour later a different woman drove on to the forecourt in a silver Jaguar. She entered the office carrying a small plastic bag, 10min's later she left and drove away. 25min's later Mr Sawyer arrived and reported the theft. A picture was on his desk and the woman in the picture was the one that had let herself in just before he arrived. As the picture was of his wedding and she was the bride, the woman in the footage was defiantly his wife.

The tray with the kettle, sugar and coffee was on a small table by the front window, I deducted she must have put the drugs in the sugar or the coffee but as I went to the tray I spotted her silver Jaguar pull up on the forecourt.

I quickly locked the door and hid in the cupboard, leaving just enough gap to see her movements. The sound of her key turning in the lock made me tingle with excitement at the thought of solving the crime. The door opened and she appeared in the doorway, the sun gleaming through her red hair draping over her shoulders. I think she had bought her imitation fur coat to match her hair, they say the most colourful things in nature are the most deadly and they are right.

The sound of her stilettos as she walked across the office echoed memories of my past years, as she approached the tray, she opened a carrier bag and my mind was fixed firmly on the present. I waited until she had put the two jars in the bag before emerging from the cupboard and introducing myself. She turned and smiled.

"I spotted your car Inspector Stewart but you won't be leaving in it."

Her hand slid into her coat pocket and pulled out a small handgun, her eyes gleamed in triumph as she raised it in my direction. In front of me was a metal three tier in tray, which I quickly grabbed and brought up in front of me as the office door slammed. As I peered over the top, Mrs Sawyer had vanished.

The sound of squealing tyres sounded from outside, but when I looked her Jaguar was still on the forecourt. I turned to put the in-tray back on the desk and there on the other side of the desk lay Mrs Sawyer, face down with the gun still in her hand. I took a tissue from the desk and carefully removed the gun from her hand. There was no pulse from her neck or wrist so I rolled her over onto her back. Her coat fell open to reveal a metal shaft protruding from her chest. For the moment, I felt the vigilante had rescued me; the truth of the matter was she was the intended victim and I was a lucky bystander.

The forensic team took the carrier bag away for analysis and I left as the coroner, Simon Watson turned up.

"Are you sure you're not the vigilante Peter? That is twice you have been only feet away when two out of the three victims have coped it, are you sure you weren't at the Lucky Gamblers Club that morning?"

"Positive, I only bet on certainties, I don't think you would find that at that club and I don't think luck would come into it. See you back at the station."

My first port of call was Carol in hope she had dug up some clue to the abduction of Jack's daughter. Tired and bleary eyed she shook her head, a migraine had set in so she went to the rest room for a lay down and close her eyes.

Sergeant Green had called in and left a message to say he had taken the chief back to his place for the night until a safe house could be found. Constable Arnold had been replaced by, Constable's White and Sky to guard Sawyer, until the morning at the hospital. Like Carol I had forgotten the time, it was 8pm so I told Carol to go home.

Her migraine was so bad she couldn't see clearly enough to drive; I said I would drive her home and pick her up the next morning.

I had never been in her apartment before and was amazed at the lovely furniture and deep pile carpets. I offered to make her a hot drink but she just wanted to put her cosy dressing gown over her blouse and skirt and curl up on top of her bed. She had a large king size bed, yet I have never known her to have a serious relationship, mind you I much prefer a double bed to a single.

As I draped her quilt over her, I noticed a picture on her bedside cabinet. The picture, had been taken when she was promoted to Inspector and me to Chief Inspector. Jack Taylor was promoted from Sergeant to Chief of police at our station. It was just the three of us in the photo, how happy we all looked. It felt like one big family since Jack took charge. I left the bedside light on, said goodnight and left.

The abduction of Ruth Lamb had made me apprehensive about leaving Grace alone so I phoned her and suggested I stayed at her place for the night. She as always sounded excited at the idea, not as excited as I was, I bet. Grace had made it like a second home to me and had bought clothes, shaver and toothbrush in fact everything I needed.

Day 4

Next morning I left to pick up Carol wondering what the day would throw at me. Day four of the case and nowhere nearer finding the killers, even though they have killed three people, none of them seem to have had a common denominator.

Carol was already dressed for work but had a cup of coffee ready; she wanted to talk over the case before leaving for work. Nothing prepared me for what she was about to say.

"Peter, you never told me that you were nearly shot yesterday, I have saved enough money to buy a small shop somewhere and we could leave the force and have a good safe life together."

I really thought all the jealous outbursts and suggestive remarks were just Carol having a laugh at my expense, she appeared to be very much in love with me even though I considered myself boring compared to others. The only thing going for me is I am easy going, dependable and loyal. I cannot dance, do not smoke or drink and a bit of a home bird. I love music, photography of wild life and write about cases I have solved. I always imagined Carol as a wild partygoer, so never took her serious. We sat in silence as we sipped our coffee and I was completely lost for words.

"Give it some thought Peter but lets get back to these killings, I only covered four of his cases before the migraine struck, I will carry on with them as soon as we get to the station, have you stumbled across any clues yet?"

Still feeling awkward and a slight lump in my throat I just shook my head. She seemed pleased with herself as we drove back to the station but by now my mind was a complete blank.

As we entered the station, a constable was standing with a woman at the main desk, apparently booking her for something. As I passed I said to Sid you don't have your dog collar on, they will have to postpone the wedding.

With that, the young woman turned and gave me a good slap across the face.

"You have just assaulted our chief Inspector, that's a serious offence."

The woman went red in the face, apologised and started trembling.

"Forget it Sid, the lady has done me a favour, don't ask, it's complicated."

Sid nodded and Carol chuckled to herself.

"Find Inspector Joe Roberts and see if he has a link between the three victims, I know he was working on the Sawyers case."

"Yes sir! And I will do some digging myself, see you later."

She only calls me sir when she is annoyed with me, still I will leave her on her own for the rest of the day while I see if Mr Sawyer has recovered.

Constable Bart White was guarding Mr Sawyer's room when I arrived and told me that Constable Brenda Sky was in his room asleep in a chair. He made sure at least one of them was fully awake so they had taken turns. He looked worried that I may have disagreed.

"Don't look so worried Constable, you have both done well, at least you both used your heads and you look after each other."

"Thank you sir, I think you know Brenda and I are getting engaged? We wondered if you would like to come to our engagement party."

"I'm not really into parties but if you don't mind me bringing a friend I would love to, I'm really happy for you both."

I left Constable White guarding the door and I entered the room, Constable Sky was fast asleep in the armchair and I wondered if Constable White knew she snored. Seeing her gave me flash backs of when I was young and hoped no one would come between him and her and ruin their young exciting love.

I had a job to reframe from laughing when I called her name. She staggered to her feet in complete disarray, red in the face she waited for my reaction.

"You young officers have done well, glad you have the task at hand, so is there anything to report."

Her young face beamed with pride, which was one wonderful feeling I seemed to have lost, as my own youth had left me.

"Apart from the night nurse, no one has been near the room, Mr Sawyer did regain conciseness about 3.30am but fell back to sleep."

"Thank you Constable, would you mind fetching a nurse or doctor to see if he can be interviewed."

By the time she returned with a doctor Mr Sawyer had come to and was staring at the ceiling.

"Mr Sawyer I am Chief Inspector Stewart, you have been poisoned, until we get the results back we can't be sure but it's a safe bet it was in your coffee."

"The alarm was still on when I arrived at work; my wife is the only one who had a key and knew the code. I had a coffee before I left the office yesterday and I was fine so are you pointing your finger at her."

"Is everything ok between you and your wife, maybe she has been a bit distant or cold towards you lately."

"I don't like your insinuations but she has been moody lately. She keeps on to me to sell the business and move to Spain. I told her over my dead body, this is my life and I would always be home-sick if we emigrated."

"Bad choice of words Mr Sawyer, over your dead body was nearly fulfilled."

"I can't believe she would go that far, I know we have started to grow apart but that's because she wants the grand life and I'm taking to long to give her that. I will get a divorce as soon as possible."

"You won't have to divorce your wife, she has been murdered, you carry on selling dodgy cars and you will be home sick, stuck in a cell for a few years and finally come out flat broke and no business."

"I never killed her, honest. I would never have hurt her, what's going on? Why would anyone want to kill her?"

"Did your wife have her fingers in any pies you know about?"

"She seemed to spend far more money than I gave her and got really angry when I queried her about where she got it."

"You have the perfect alibi for the time of your wife's murder, I will be in touch with you again and I may have a few more questions."

I must be honest; it did cross my mind that these murders could be the work of hired killers. Until we catch them I must assume he is innocent.

As I left, I told constables Sky and White that I would send someone to relive them, even though I was convinced that Sawyer was not a target.

I had just reached my car when a nurse who was out of breath approached me,

"Chief Inspector we have just had a call from your office, they want you to go to the free-church on the common urgently."

"Thank you nurse, are they still on the phone."

"Yes, they said they will stay on the line to see if I managed to catch you."

"Can you tell them I am on my way and ask them to get someone to relive my two constables as they have been there all night?"

The nurse nodded and I drove off to the church.

As I drove up the drive towards the church, Carol and two paramedic's, were leaning against the ambulance with their arms crossed looking impatient. Carol beckoned to me and disappeared into the church. She stopped at the altar and pointed towards a pew with a vicar sitting on it.

The vicar's eyes were open but he was as dead as a doornail, yes, there was a steel bolt sticking out of his chest.

"Why would anyone murder a vicar? Who found him Carol?"

"The florist who brings fresh flowers, funny thing is she has never seen him before, the paramedic's gave her a sedative, she's, asleep in the ambulance."

"We have got to search the church and grounds, I have a feeling we will find the original vicar, I just hope he is still alive."

We searched the church and the bell tower but found nothing.

"Unless I'm mistaken Carol most of the churches have a cellar and the door is probably outside."

At the rear of the church we found some steps leading down to a door, it was a solid oak door and locked.

"There is no way we can break it in Peter, it must be 2inch's thick."

"We may not have to; give me that big brick in the corner."

"Ok but you will never break in with that. How did you know the key was under it? I know it was tilted."

We entered and lucky for us a flick of the light switch and the whole cellar lit up. Even with the lights, the passageways gave you a very eerie feeling and we stuck together as we weaved our way through the cellar. It was like a rabbit warren with passageways leading off in different directions.

"We are going to get lost down here Peter, I don't like it."

"I will scratch an arrow on the walls to show us the way back."

"You won't have to look someone has beaten you to it."

She was right we followed the arrows, which led us to a locked door and the key was hanging on the doorframe on a nail. Inside we found the real vicar with a head wound. Carol rushed back to get the paramedics who by this time were complaining about being kept hanging about but suddenly snapped into an efficient duo eager to put their expert abilities to work. They were happy as they declared the vicar although unconscious had a superficial wound. The vicar was on the stretcher, being weaved along the passageways, Carol, and I noticed some cardboard box's in the corner of the room. We were both staring at the boxes as I was running my penknife along one eager to find out its contents. Inside were vicar's robes and dog collars, in another box we found large candles about two inches thick and four feet long, the type used at the side on the altar.

"I thought we were going to find drugs Peter, still at least we saved the vicar."

I took hold of the wick on one of the candles to pull it out of the box but the wick pulled out and was only two inches long. After pulling the candle out of the box, I broke it in half over my knee, which nearly brought tears to my eyes. Inside was a long 1.5inch round tube nearly the length of the candle.

I pulled the cork out of it and inside it was full of white powder.

"Better phone Sergeant Linden, looks like heroin but I can't be sure but he will."

We made our way back to the altar after locking the cellar door and waited for Simon Watson the coroner to arrive with Sergeant Linden.

"When I arrived here I noticed four cars and the ambulance, one is yours so the others must have been the florist, vicar and the dead man. With luck if we find out which is his we can identify him."

"That's easy Peter it's got to be the expensive big Rover."

"Ok, phone it through and see what they come back with."

She did and it was registered to the florist. The dead man's car was a mark two Cortina estate in showroom condition.

"You seem to have known the rover wasn't his car the way you smiled at me."

"He would have had to have an estate car to bring all those box's and as the florist comes every morning and the bogus vicar only appeared this morning I would imagine the dead man brought the boxes this morning."

"I hate you sometimes Chief Inspector Stewart, you could have told me."

"Perhaps you can let me know the name of the dead man and anything else you found out. I know the original vicar is Julian Tap."

Carol phoned the office while I checked around the dead body.

"Peter! The car is registered to a Mr Harry Barrow he had been caught for drug smuggling and dealing in Wales, but the witness was a victim of a hit and run. Barrow was acquitted then he disappeared. The Welsh police have been trying to track him down as a new witness had come forward."

"I would like to know how the killers knew he would be here; they must have known he was not the normal vicar, what if the victim was meant to be Julian Tap. We need to get forensics to check those boxes, to see if Tap's fingerprints are on the box containing the candles, he may have been an accomplice."

"Let's get back to the office Peter and I will contact the Welsh police to fax us Barrow's picture and anything else they have on him."

"Good idea Carol, I will leave you to have a word with forensics and I will meet you back at the station."

"You used your left hand so don't forget my bar of chocolate."

"You really study my little ways, are there any other ones you haven't told me about?"

"See you later Peter I will have a word with Henry Waters about the fingerprints. A big bar would be nice seeing I'm doing your leg work."

I arrived at the station and phoned the hospital to see when I could talk to the vicar. He was stable but they have not been able to wake him and told me to phone again late in the evening. I sent Constable Arnold alias -The Mammoth - to keep guard on the vicar.

Inspector Joe Roberts stood in front of my desk shaking his head as he watched me eat my bar of chocolate and sip my black coffee.

"Carry on like that Peter old boy and we will have to buy you a park bench to sit on. I can't figure out how you stay slim, anyway I have been busy leaning on some of my contacts and it would appear all three victims were pedalling drugs, that is the only common denominator I have dug up."

"We have four victims now, I think you should get to the free church on the common before our team's finish up, tell them I sent you."

"I'm on my way, thanks chief you're a gem. Hi Carol sorry can't stop."

"Where's Joe off to in such a hurry."

"He found out all three victims were into drugs in one way or another, he was unaware of the incident at the church so that's where I've sent him. Three heads are better than two on a case like this especially seeing we haven't a clue to the identities of the killers. Your bar of chocolate is on your desk."

"Thank you oh generous one, I will carry on looking through Jack Taylor's cases to see if I can find something, do you want to help?"

"The killers may have kidnapped his daughter knowing we would take this route just to waste our time, you carry on digging just in case it's not a red herring and I will join Joe Roberts and visit some more of his contacts."

As I was leaving the office, our typist Sally Trent handed me an envelope.

"The Welsh police have just faxed the information you requested."

"Thanks Sally I will look at it with Inspector Forward."

We were knocked back when the sheets slid out of the envelope onto Carols desk, on the top was the photo of Harry Barrow. The dead man in the church was not him, I contacted the welsh police straight away to warn them he was still on the loose. I had a picture sent to them through the fax machine in the hope they could identify the dead man. While we waited for a reply we looked at the dossiers they had sent, I spotted a man associated with him living in Cranbrook Kent. Carol started to check to see if the man was on our files, before she had typed it into the computer my phone rang, it was Inspector Roberts ringing to tell me that the dead man was Carl Jenkins not Harry Barrow. Apparently, Joe had questioned him once after Sergeant Linden had raided his home looking for an assignment of drugs, but no drugs were found at his property.

I wondered if the killers mistook him for Harry Barrow as we had, if they had and they read in the newspaper that they had killed the wrong man, Barrow would probably be the next one to turn up dead. My mind was always working overtime and the thought crossed my mind that Barrow could be behind the killings but why leave the candles full of drugs at the church. Sergeant Linden entered the office and told me we had identified the wrong man. The drugs found in the church in his estimation would be worth at least £2 million on the streets. No drug dealer would leave that behind so I would have to assume Barrow was not behind the killings.

"Tell me Sergeant Linden, do you know any of Carl Jenkins associates."

"You would have to ask Inspector Roberts, I only organise the raids and I do remember the woman on site when we broke in. She was a lovely woman, long raven black hair very pretty."

"Pull your self together Sergeant your drooling at the mouth."

"Sorry chief I was just remembering. Her name was Julie Black; Inspector Roberts interviewed her so he will have her address."

"Thank you Sergeant any lead will help. Carol contact Joe and tell him I need him back here straight away, you stay at your desk while I take Jack Taylor's case files up to him, I understand constable Arnold drove him into work today, something might jog his memory."

The chief was pleased to be able to help; I think he misses being a Sergeant and gets a bit bored stuck up there in his office.

   After leaving the chiefs office I went to the staff room to get a coffee for Carol and myself. We sat and had our coffee while we waited for Joe to arrive. Carol's proposal was still clouding my mind so I found it difficult to have a general conversation with her.

"Did you contact Joe Carol?"

"He was already on his way back and he thinks he may have a lead."

"He may have remembered Julie Black, see if you can find an address for her."

"I will have to pull the files of the raid I will need her date of birth at least."

I watched as she walked out of the office and wondered why an attractive and exciting woman like Carol would even look at me twice. Several men at the station have asked her out and been turned down, being a black belt in judo and brown belt in karate no one pushes their luck.

Joe and Carol arrived back in the office at the same time, the lead Joe had thought of was, Carl Jenkins had a boat moored at Tonbridge, which was also raided on the same day. According to Joe, Julie Black was living with her mother at the time of the raid and only stayed at Carl Jenkins place at the weekends as she worked Monday to Friday.

"I think the chief needs an airing so why not invite him to go with you and check on that boat. Carol and I will try and find Julie Black; she may be able to give us some names of Jenkins friends."

"O.k. Pete, is it alright if I tell the chief you suggested that he accompanies me?"

"Of course but you better get a move on; by the time you get there daylight will be fading, take a couple of torches just in case."

Joe went to see the chief and Carol did her magic on the computer, a few minutes later someone whistled from the doorway, I looked and there stood the chief with a big smile on his face giving me the thumbs up before rushing off in pursuit of Joe.

"I have it Peter, at least her mothers address, shall we set off?"

"Why not it may give us something to sleep on, don't look at me like that I was talking about clues not Julie black, if it wasn't for the fact you would beat me up I'd put you over my knee and give you a good spanking."

"Oh please Peter I promise I won't struggle."

"I can't win, your terrible, let's hit the road."

Carol insisted she drove, as she knew the way to Frittenden and had found the house on the internet.

By the time we arrived, it was starting to get dark, as the cottage was on the outskirts of the village and shrouded with trees, it looked quite forbidding. Our headlights exposed a green Ford Orion in front of the cottage.

"Some one must be in Peter the light is on in the back room, let's peek through the side widow."

Before I could stop her, she was creeping down the side of the cottage towards the light in the window, she was peering in the window when I started down the side of the wall, I stopped in my tracks when a loud barking echoed through the chilly night air. Carol was soon with me at the front door and I rang the doorbell. A middle-aged woman opened the door and we introduced ourselves.

Once seated in the living room she asked to keep our voices down because her mother was asleep.

I nearly asked who was loudest, the dog or us? Apparently it was a recording connected to a motion detector. Julie was devastated to learn Jenkins had been murdered.

"I thought the world of him; he wasn't a bad man he just got involved with that creep from down south, the first time I knew what he had got involved in was when some of your colleges raided his place. I work as a nurse and I see the pain and suffering drugs cause so I gave him a choice the drugs or me. The money that creep gave him turned his head. The creeps name was Barrow and when Carl was out he turned up and tried it on with me, I hit him with Carl's Toby mug and locked myself in the bedroom, I never told Carl because of his temper and the fact Barrow had a gun. After the incident Barrow started taking Carl to Soho, that's when I finished with him."

"Have you any information about their other friends or places they frequently visited, inspector Forward can jot down anything at all that might help us catch him, even an insignificant thing could help."

"Carl has or had a boat moored at Tonbridge but I only went there with him nearly two years ago, so I wouldn't know how to find it again, if he still has it."

"We are checking that out as we speak, can you remember anything at all, did he start changing his habits or apart from Soho visit other places?"

"He started acting weird because he suddenly went religious, not that he started reading the

Bible but he spent a lot of time at a church on the outskirts of Tunbridge Wells, or so he told me."
"Do you know the name of the church or the location?"
"All he ever said was he was going to church and when I asked if it was the local one he said it was near Tunbridge Wells. I'm sorry but I have to get ready for work, one thing, Barrow he drives a Cortina estate but has turned up in a black Mustang sometimes, I really must get ready for work."
I thanked her and we left, Carol said she would drop me off at my place, which she did, then pick me up the next morning. I gave Grace a bell to say goodnight to make sure she was ok. I had just snuggled down in my bed when there was a loud banging on my front door. Slipping into my bathrobe, I reached the front door and called to ask who was there.
"It's me Carol let me in, I can't go back to my flat they tried to kill me, quick let me in hurry please hurry."
She shot pass me as I opened the front door slamming it shut as she turned.
"I was only two streets away from my flat when a car started to overtake me, next thing I know it swerved into the side of my car sending me into a garden, thankfully it was open plan so I reversed and came straight here."
"You can't stay here, how about you stay with Grace like you did before she wouldn't mind."
"Have you seen the time, I will sleep on the settee if you don't want me in your bed, is that alright Mr Chief Inspector Stewart?"

"Sleep in my bed by all means and I will sleep on the settee, anymore bickering and you can get your backside back to your flat."

"I love it when you get all masterful Mr Peter Stewart; the settee is yours, is it ok to have a shower and grab a shirt out of your wardrobe."

"It's an on-suit so see you in the morning and heaven help you if you answer the phone, I will have you down graded back down to a constable and that's a promise so goodnight, help yourself to the kitchen if you need anything."

I settled down and soon fell asleep on the settee.

Day 5

After breakfast we set off to the yard after inspecting the damage to her car, it had a dent in the front wing at the back of the headlight and a smear of red paint.

When we arrived at the station, we reported it to Sid on the front desk. He started to laugh.

"Come with me Carol, I will show your would be killer."

Ted Reed was in charge of the cells and seemed to laugh along with Sid when Sid told him of the dangerous killer in his cell. The cell door swung open to reveal an old woman fast asleep on the bunk bed. Sid turned and said.

"Sorry Inspector Forward you were just in the wrong place at the wrong time, Miss Marsh here fell asleep at the wheel and said she seemed to hit something that woke her up, she claims she looked in her mirror but she was the only car on the road. Her son is on his way to pick her up."

"The reason she was the only car on the road was she shot me into someone's garden, I hope she's insured."

"She is and she turned up here late last night as she was worried she had hit someone or something, her tablets had got mixed up and made her drowsy. Ted Reed drove to where she claimed the incident took place and found nothing and he also checked out the hospitals."

"If she is happy to pay the bill when I have it repaired I won't take it any further. I admire her for seeking help and not just going home. Thanks to Miss Marsh I had a very memorable evening." Sid and Ted looked puzzled as Carol walked off looking pleased with herself.

After getting a coffee, I sat at my desk wondering how I was going trace the church Miss Black had mentioned when Joe entered the office and came over to me.

"The chief won't be in today he slipped on the boat and twisted his ankle. The hospital patched him up and I took him home, I left old bulldozer with him just in case you are right about him being at risk. Sergeant Green will be replaced by Constables Sky and White tonight."

"Carol said you had a lead, if you mean Julie Black we have already traced and talked to her. She only knew of a church near Tunbridge wells, Soho and the boat Jenkins and Barrow visited."

"Jenkins never told her he had another property at Westerham and kept a lover there. I would like to take Sergeant Linden and his armed squad to that address, Barrow was always after Jenkins girlfriends so it's a good bet he is shacked up at the love nest at Westerham."

"Julie Black told us he carries a gun and he tried getting off with her I can't give you the go ahead, Jack Taylor being the chief will be glad to."

One phone call to the chief and Joe started to organise the raid.

Carol put out a bulletin for locations of any black Mustangs spotted, she had checked with DVLA and no vehicle had been registered under Harry Barrow.

I was amazed at how many churches there were in and around Tunbridge Wells and how far into the weald Tunbridge Wells council stretched. What made the task harder was Tonbridge, Sevenoaks and Crowborough councils bordered within three miles of Tunbridge Well central. A joint decision was to draw a three-mile circle round the centre of the town and concentrate on the churches within that area. By the time we had it all sorted it was nearly midday, before we set off we went to the canteen for lunch. Carol had a lovely figure but I couldn't finish my lunch due to the amount of food she was getting through.

As we were finishing our coffee Miss Trend our interpreter came in to tell me she had answered my telephone, the call was from one of our traffic cops, Constable Philips.

"Constable Philips wants you to meet him urgently at the Free Church on the common, he has located the black Mustang and there are two dead bodies. Constable Arnold has also left a message just to let you know the vicar is awake when you want to talk to him."

"Thanks Sally, I will take Carol with me to meet Constable Philips, if you could let Constable Arnold know I will be there later."

Carol and I headed back to the church both trying to guess who the two dead people were. Constable Philips stopped us at the entrance to the drive and told us to follow him along the road. A track six hundred yards further along the road led up into a wood ending at a woodcutting shed. The black Mustang car was parked along side and going by the picture the Welsh police had sent, Barrow was lying a few feet away with a steel bolt sticking out of his chest but under his arm.

"The other one is over there sir against that pile of logs."

I glanced in the direction he was pointing, slumped against the bottom of the pile was the infamous dwarf. His lethal little crossbow was still in his hand.

"How did you manage to find them way up here in the woods?"

"We had an anonymous phone call from someone claiming to be a walker."

I inspected the dwarf visually and could see a blood stain under his jacket; a hole was in the middle of the stain indicating a bullet wound. Trouble was there was no gun near Barrow; although the position of the bodies indicated he had pulled his gun when he spotted the crossbow turned and side on to extend his arm for an accurate shot. Thy must have both pulled their triggers at the same time.

"I think it's fairly obvious they killed each other but where is Barrows gun and how did the dwarf get right out here."

"I agree Peter there must have been a third person, probably the woman."

"The woman would have taken her friend with her and why take the gun and not the crossbow. The dwarf must have killed the bogus vicar at the church and arranged to meet Barrow on the pretence of buying drugs."

"So how did the dwarf get here and who took the gun."

"If you look at Barrows left hand he still has his car keys. The friend Barrow brought with him must have panicked and finding no keys in Barrows car took the dwarfs, although their legs would be a bit cramped."

"Makes sense, to trace the car we have to find the identity of the little man and the woman will really make someone pay for killing him, he's quite cute."

"Maybe so but he was still a cold blooded killer, as to the third person who left this scene forensics Should get fingerprints and DNA from the car, check his pockets."

"Don't forget the dwarf's accomplice may have brought the little guy in her car."

Carol carefully searched his pockets, you could see the motherly look in her face when she looked at the dwarf, I must admit I felt sad looking at the little figure.

As Carol pulled a folded piece of paper from inside his jacket pocket, our forensics man Henry Waters drove up closely followed by Simon

Watson the coroner. Simon stood looking at the two bodies scratching his head while Henry flashed away with his camera.

"Look at this Peter he had this list of names in his pocket and you won't believe who is on it."

"Let me have a look at the list. Inspector Saunders! But! He's doing time, we had better let the prison warden know and check the names on here they haven't killed yet. They are all well known crooks, trouble is if we warn them they are likely to get trigger happy and kill innocent people."

"Ask Waters if it's ok to check Barrows pockets seeing he's finished taking his pictures and check the rest of the dwarf's pockets."

Henry Waters insisted he check the pockets in case we disturbed vital evidence. Barrow had his wallet and lighter, his cigarettes were in his car, some change in his pocket and his watch was missing which was obvious by the lack of sunburn in the shape of the watch. All the dwarf had apart from the list of names were a pack of chewing gum, a penknife and a padlock key.

We thanked the lads and decided to go to the hospital and question the vicar.

Constable Arnold was pleased to see us and said we were wasting our time as the vicar was sitting in a pew reading the bible then came to in the hospital.

The vicar was sitting up in bed cupping a mug of tea in his hands, the bandages made him look like he was wearing a turban.

"Hello Vicar I am Chief Inspector Stewart and this is Inspector Forward, I understand from

Constable Arnold you never got a look at your attackers but perhaps you can tell me if you had a box of clothes and dog collars in the basement, have you noticed any strangers lately?"

"As far as I know the cellar was empty and the main boiler was the only reason I ventured down there, the passageways stretch for quite away, it's like maize down there and I nearly got lost when I first took over. I can't say I have seen any strangers, just the engineer to look at the boiler I was having breakfast when he turned up. He was not the usual one but he seemed ok, so I just gave him the keys and told him to leave them under the mat of the pew next the alter, I should have asked for his identity card."

"In this case it was a good job you didn't; we hope you soon feel better and thank you for your help."

"Well what's the next move peter? Nothing seems to be straight forward, in fact I feel completely lost."

"I am sure the vicar is not in danger so if we send Constable Arnold and Inspector Roberts to check out the rest of the church cellar we will start on the list, in fact they have been working their way down the list, Gary Simpson is the next on the list. He runs a betting shop so we should be able to keep him under surveillance."

"Does that mean I have to spend most of the day sitting in the car with you?"

Constable Arnold laughed.

"I hope your up on your self defence chief, good luck, I will round up Inspector Roberts and check out that spooky cellar."

Carol went red in the face. She looked at me and said.

"Well don't just stand there grinning lets see if we can save Garry Simpson."

We took two flasks of black coffee and some cheese sandwiches with us and set off thinking we were one-step ahead. As we were getting in the car Constable Philips pulled across the front of us.

"Simon Watson is in casualty, he was clubbed over the head while putting the bodies in his van, when he came to the dwarf's body was gone."

"What about the other body? Has anyone been assigned to bring the body and Simon's van back?"

"I have left a constable to bring coroner Simon Watson back from the hospital or take him home and Constable Arnold is bringing the body and van back being followed by Inspector Roberts."

"You've all done well and as you have every thing in hand we will stop off at the hospital to see Simon then set off to the bookies."

On the way Carol phoned the hospital to inquire about our coroner, they told her one of our officers had taken him home.

We went straight to the bookies and decided to go in and place a small bet. As I placed the bet, I enquired if Mr Simpson was on site.

"If you want to see the boss you will have to come back tomorrow or leave a message, he's at his other shop today in London, are you sure about this bet, either you're an idiot or a rookie, it doesn't stand a chance."

"Your right I am a rookie at gambling, it's the first and last one I'll place."

I gave Carol the ticket just in case miracles do happen and went back to the car to phone our colleges in London and ask them to check on Simpson. To save time I decided to pay a call on Mrs Simpson and enquire what time she expected her husband home.

"How would I know, he comes home all hours of the day and sometimes not till the next day, if you're a friend of his clear off, I put the trash in the dustbin I don't have it stand on my doorstep." Before I could explain, she slammed the door in my face. Carol burst into laughter.

"You should see your face Peter I wish I had my camera, what a picture."

"I can't believe it, I never saw that coming, wonder were he goes all night."

"Soho where all you dirty old men go, where else."

"I have never been there and I suppose I'm just old fashioned in that respect."

"Sorry that was uncalled for, anyway I like the idea spending the night with you but not stuck in a car, I want a nice shower and curl up in bed."

"Your right it's getting dark and he could be at Soho or in a gambling game, let me drop you off home and we can come back first thing in the morning."

After dropping Carol off, I called on Grace for a cup of coco. She opened the shop door as that was the only access to her flat and said.

"Thank you darling she was very kind and stayed for a bite to eat, you are thoughtful and I'm sorry I couldn't join you and Carol at the pub but just after your constable left I had to rush to the loo with upset tummy."

"I never sent a woman constable round and never went to any pub, what did she look like and did you get her name?"

"She was quite distinctive, you must know her, she has a foreign accent and a lovely lock of jet black hair, she has a different shape to her nose but I can't remember what you call it, she was quite pretty."

"The word your looking for is a Roman nose, what are they playing at, first Jacks daughter now you. Constable Sky can stay with you in the day and we will spend the evenings and nights together, here or my place."

Grace went white as a sheet and passed out into my arms. I felt so helpless and useless, she could have been killed while I was trying to save some no good crooks life. I will have to try to approach this case from a different angle and do the unexpected. We went back to my house but Grace kept waking me up through the night thinking she heard noises.

Day 6

The Morning finally arrived and luckily, I woke before the alarm went off as Grace was still out for the count. After I had a coffee and a bowl of cereal I phoned Sid on the main desk, I asked him to send constable Sky over to my place as soon as possible. I phoned Carol and updated her with the events so far.

It was 8am when I heard Grace call my name and the sound of her bare feet echoing across the landing.

"I'm here sweetheart come down and have some breakfast."

She appeared in the doorway looking concerned and deep in thought.

"Mothballs!" she called out.

"What on earth are you talking about? Constable Sky will be here shortly; perhaps you should forget the shop for today and rest here."

"The bogus police woman she smelt of mothballs and grease paint, I know the smell because my friend was in a play and used it."

"We have been looking for a woman with a roman nose, if you're right it's probably false."

"Her accent was wrong in the respect that it sounded as if she couldn't make up her mind which one to use. There was something else, while I was admiring her jet-black hair I felt puzzled by something and now I know what. Her eye brows were brunette, if you want my advice my lovely Peter look in the theatres."

"I was coming to the same conclusion, you may have saved us a lot of wasted time and some lives, what do you want for breakfast?"

As I made Grace her scrambled egg on toast, my gut feeling was working overtime again.

Churning all the clues Grace had just given me, over and over in my mind made me think, an actor would never make such obvious mistakes.

"Tell me Sweetheart where did your friend get her grease paint and accessories?"

"I think they were supplied by the theatre and they would have bought them from a supplier or a fancy costume shop."

"That's what I though, and I feel that it is from one of these shops our killers are using as their base."

"That sounds like constable Sky has arrived do you want me to answer the door."

"Not in your underwear Grace I will answer it." Constables Sky and White stood on the doorstep looking pleased with them selves.

"Morning sir we came as soon as possible."

"I only asked for you constable Sky, you two aren't married yet, anyway have a seat in the front room while Miss Day finishes her breakfast, when she has finished you can help yourselves to a cuppa." Constable White remarked.

"Our chief said it would be ok if I came, he just wants to get this case solved."

When Grace disappeared upstairs, I told the two lovebirds to help themselves to refreshments in the kitchen and practise being married by doing the washing up.

After saying goodbye to Grace, I set off to pick up Inspector Forward.

Unlike myself, Carol is on the internet and had made a list of outlets selling grease paint and theatrical accessories. She seemed to be in a very chirpy mood and very pleased with herself.

"Wow! Carol you are in a good mood today, have you had some good news?"

"I have a date tonight with an old friend, he has made good and works in the city. He said he would pick me up in his stretch limo, he emailed his picture and he is really handsome."

I must admit it I felt really jealous and annoyed but why I have the woman of my dreams Gracie.

Trying not to show my feelings, I said.

"I'm very pleased for you, grab the list and we can get going."

She seemed a bit disappointed that I never tried to talk her out of her date.

The outlets were miles apart, by midday we had only called on three.

On the way to the fourth, which was on the outskirts of London we pulled over to a quaint little café for a bite to eat.

After we had devoured a baked potato loaded with cheese and accompanied with salad, we sat drinking our black coffees I couldn't resist saying.

"You'll be eating something a bit more special tonight, in a lovely restaurant, being swept you off your feet."

I wish I had kept my mouth shut, she just looked a bit sad and carried on drinking her coffee.

On the way to the loo, I noticed a poster advertising a funfair including sideshows, one being -The Remarkable Archer-. I called Carol over who shrugged her shoulders.

"Seems a bit convenient, still it's worth a try as Farnborough is only about seven miles away."

It was 1.35pm when we finally found the funfair.

If I had read the poster properly, I would have known it opens at 5pm.

"There is no one about Peter, let's knock on some of the caravans."

"Don't do that Miss, they sleep till 2.30pm, can I help as they are never getting to sleep till the early hours."

"I am inspector Forward and this is Chief Inspector Stewart, we need to talk to The Remarkable Archer."

"Join the club; they disappeared about a week ago when her husband was killed."

"Did they have a dwarf in the act?"

"You must be talking about Timmy Strong, he did take part in the act sometimes but he disappeared after the funeral same time as Anna Lextor, Jerry Lextor's wife. Jerry was the archer although Anna and Timmy used a crossbow."

"How did Mr Lextor die?"

"I told you he was killed when he went to book an act, Timmy was with him when he was killed but managed to escape."

"Did they give a clue to why and who killed Mr Lextor?"

"Timmy said Jerry, must have seen something he shouldn't because he opened the main door to the club where he was asked to do his act, next thing Timmy knew a shot rang out and Jerry fell backwards dead."

"I think you have cleared up the motive but did he say where and the name of the club he was hoping to work at."

"He didn't say but he had an insane look in his eyes they were all very close. If you find him tell him there's always a job here for him."

"I'm afraid Mr Strong is dead, thank you for your help. By the way did Mrs Lextor have a Roman nose?"

"No she is a really pretty woman, slim with shoulder length mousey hair; I can't believe little Timmy is dead."

We left the man to his grief and headed back to the police station. It was clear now why they started the killing spree; if they kill all the main crooks, they are certain to kill the ones responsible for Mr Lextor's murder.

"How come we weren't aware of his murder Peter?"

"That's what's puzzling me, if Timmy Strong ran for his life how did they get his body and who signed the death certificate; the doctor or coroner would certainly inform us if a bullet was the cause of death."

"I will try and see if Mrs Lextor had any relatives that may be giving her refuge. At least we know the identity of the killers."

When we returned to the station, Carol got to work on her computer while I went to see our coroner Simon Watson. He knew nothing about the shooting but said he would phone other coroners from other areas, as the man at the fair hadn't given any clue to where the shooting took place.

To save me time I rang the police at Orpington and asked if they could send one of their officers to the fair to see if anyone there hade a picture of Mrs Lextor. As I finished the phone call, Carol came skipping over to my desk.

"Fancy taking me to Bexhill chief inspector Stewart?"

"Why would I want to do that inspector Forward? Apart from Grace, we have enough to worry about trying to solve this case."

"Well if you can't be bothered to follow up a lead I will delete her brother's address, which happens to be at Bexhill his name is Gerry Tanner."

"Fancy a stick of rock Inspector Forward or in your case a big bag of chips?"

"I think I would like both chief inspector Stewart."

"Times getting on, we can make an early start in the morning. Perhaps you can print all the information on Lextor and her brother then I will drop you off early so you can get ready for your date, you don't want to be late."

Carol printed the info off and put it in a big envelope, which I took with us to save coming back to station in the morning.

"Where is he taking you on your date Carol, somewhere special I bet?"

"We booked at the Primrose Restaurant, a bit pricey but he said I'm worth it."

I sat there not saying a word, not that I was jealous, well maybe a little, I knew the restaurant had been closed for over a week for refurbishment, it was not due to reopen for another ten days.

"What's the matter Peter; you're not jealous are you? I've bought a sexy dress for tonight and sexy underwear just in case I get lucky."

 I never had the heart to say anything.

"He's a very lucky chap, off you go."

 I watched her until she shut her front door, as I went to drive off I spotted the envelope, my curiosity got the better of me so I turned the engine off and decided to have a look. I started to read and noticed Carols light on in her flat, the information Carol had printed off showed that neither Mrs Lextor nor her brother had been in trouble with the law, Mr Lextor however had been convicted of grievous bodily harm to his first wife. Carol had been very thorough in gathering the information but there was no mention of a divorce. Still engrossed in the info I spotted Carols light go off in her flat. I suddenly realised she would see me still parked there and come to the conclusion I was spying on her.

I reversed up the road and parked behind a car so I could finish reading. I was curious to see her outfit so I did watch but she never appeared. I finished reading and drove home.

I was pleased to get home early and it would be a nice surprise for Grace. I was surprised to see Constable Sky's car had gone but thought Constable White may have gone off in it. I was about fifty yards from my house when I pulled over as I spotted a man leaving my house after receiving a kiss and a hug by Grace. I watched as the man walked over to a taxi then throwing a kiss to Grace the taxi disappeared up the road.

I was convinced it was all innocent but how did he know Grace was staying at my place. I let myself in and decided to go straight upstairs to my bedroom and get a change of clothes. To my surprise, Gracc was making the bed and she looked shocked to see me.

"What are you doing back this early? I didn't expect you back for another two hours; I will get you some dinner in a minute.

"I made the bed this morning while you were making breakfast and where are Constables Sky and White?"

"I pulled the covers back after you left to air the bed and I told them they could go as I wanted to be alone for the rest of the evening."

"How long ago did they leave and why did you want to be on your own?"

"I sent them off about one and a half hours ago and just wanted to be alone."

"Sorry I came home early, so you've been on your own since they left."

"I know but it was nice just being here alone reading a book."

I felt confused and apart from a migraine building up, my chest felt like a bag of old brick rubble. I couldn't sleep with her again until I found out why she had lied. Perhaps I should have asked her outright but as she had already lied.

I needed to get out of the house.

"I have only come back for a change of clothes; we have a stake out so I will be back about 8am when I'm relived by someone else."

"I will get you a coffee and some sandwiches; oh I had better take the laundry basket down and put the washing on."

I'll get it; you make the coffee and sandwiches."

She went red in the face and disappeared out the bedroom leaving a trail of scent behind her. I felt gutted when I looked at the laundry basket which held all the tell tale signs of my worst fears.

I left the basket where it was and had a change of cloths then left without saying a word. As I drove away, Grace felt like a stranger in my mind and all the love and happiness seemed to blow away in the wind.

The only friend I could trust in the world was Carol so I thought I would give her a ring and tell her to meet me at Bexhill. I thought I would get a room at one of the bed and breakfast places. Expecting to leave a message on her answer phone, I rang her number. When I got to the bit about meeting her there she picked up the phone.

"What's up Peter you sound upset? pop round for a coffee and a chat."

"I'm not going to spoil your date so I will meet you there."

"What date, I only want you so please come and talk, don't worry I know you and Grace are in love, I will behave myself."

I felt light headed and confused so the thought of driving to Bexhill in my state of mind seemed to taxing; Carol's couch seemed much more welcome.

The front door opened and there stood Carol in her dressing gown, bare legs slippers and a cheeky expression on her pretty face.

"Sorry carol I've stopped you getting ready for your date."

"I told you I made it all up I was just off to bed, come in and tell me what's up. You look terrible and why aren't you spending the night with Grace?"

I told her everything that had happed; she just gave me a kiss on the cheek then disappeared into the kitchen. She came back with two hot chocolates and sat at the dining table where I joined her.

"You don't seem surprised Carol, what are you not telling me."

"I know I shouldn't have but I ran a check on her, she had been married before and don't worry she was divorced by her husband. After the divorce she reverted to her maiden name. I traced her ex and met up with him.

The reason he divorced her was she was mad on an ex flame, he would just turn up out of the blue and seemed to have her under a spell. He would have a brief fling with her then disappear. Her husband forgave her once but seven months later it happened again, so he divorced Grace. It would seem that Romeo is back on the scene.

"Looks like I'm even more boring in bed if she needs more than I can give her."

"What are you going to do, I couldn't tell you before or you would think I wanted to break you two up and have you for myself."

"If I am that boring in bed you had better find someone else as well."

"If you have finished with Grace, let's see how boring you are in bed."

She took off her dressing gown revealing a black sexy satin negligee.

"I bought this when I found out about Bill Turner and Grace. I got it in the hope we would soon spend the night together."

She took my hand and led me into her bedroom.

Day 7

Next morning at breakfast, Carol said I was wonderful in bed and hoped I felt the same about her. I told her I was amazed at my stupidity at not seeing how compatible we were and how young she made me feel.

As we were getting ready to leave for Bexhill I received a message on my mobile, it was from Grace. –I HAVE GONE HOME, I AM SORRY FOR EVERYTHING, PERHAPS WE CAN STILL BE FRIENDS GRACE X.-

I just couldn't bring myself to answer it; I showed Carol the text, which brought a big smile to her pretty little face.

"Its official then your free, let's get to Bexhill."

I thought it a good idea to let Carol drive as my mind was still in turmoil. As she drove, I kept looking at her, she is so full of energy and very attractive, I guess that is why I kept her at bay so I wouldn't get hurt.

We arrived at Bexhill and the brother's address was easy to find.

After introducing ourselves he invited us in, according to him he had cut all ties with his sister once she married. Mr Lextor was according to him a nasty bit of work and she would be stuck in a caravan following a fair, he considered she was just throwing her life away. He refused to believe she was capable of murder so we thanked him and left.

After spending last night together we were like a couple of walking along the beach and throwing pebbles in the sea, one good thing about the coast the chip shops are open nearly all day. Carol had her cod and chips while I had cheesy chips. I was half way through mine as Carol was just finishing hers. She certainly had an appetite and I don't just mean food, not that I'm complaining.

I had a black coffee and Carol downed two large chocolate milk shakes.

"Are you sure you haven't got worms Carol? The only one I have known to shovel food down like that was the ex mother-in-law."

"I hope you haven't played any more pranks on her lately, Sid can't keep hiding her complaints she makes to the station about the childish prankster."

"Hang on I've got a call from Jack the chief, Yes we found her brother and we will be on our way back shortly, oh! When? Ok."

"What's up? What did he say? You look shocked."

"The bookie Gary Simpson coped it as he was locking up his shop last night."

"Why did they wait till now to tell you?"

I turned off my mobile last night on the way to you; until we were having breakfast; they kept phoning my home until Sergeant Kemp told the chief where we had gone."

"That's one a day and there is another five on the list, we must have missed a clue, how on earth are we going to stop them?"

"We had better get back Carol, did you trace Timmy Strong's car?"

"He hadn't got a car; sorry I forgot to tell you, is it important?"

"Yes because that means Harry Barrow had someone with him, when we get to the station I want you to find anyone that worked with Barrow, providing the killer doesn't beat us to him, in-fact he may even be on the list."

Once back at the station Carol headed for her computer and Inspector Joe Roberts who had been involved in checking on Garry Simpson, who was suspected of laundering stolen money.
I headed for Jack Taylor's office to get an update.
"Hello chief we are back and Mrs Lextor's brother had broken all ties with her once she married Lextor, apparently a nasty piece of work."
"Things are looking bad for us and if we have not solved the case soon head office will send others in to take over."
"Were there any witness's to the killing last night chief?"
"Take a look at the hit list and guess who was driving by the bookies when Simpson was killed."
"By the tone of your voice I take it must have been Terry Pearson the next one on the list, did he get a description? Or was he spotted by someone."
"You caught on quick, no he came into the station trembling like a leaf and Sergeant Kemp thought he was dreaming when he saw one of the hardest men in the district standing the other side of the reception desk trembling with fright."
"What goes round comes round as they say, the pain and suffering that man has inflicted on his victims over the years makes me feel like killing him myself."
"I know your frustration Peter and that could be what's driving the vigilante. Pearson claimed it

was a kid that fired the bolt into Simpson, that piece of trash is so scared he said if we protect him till the killer is caught he will confess to the crimes we have trying to book him for."

"You must be joking? If he confessed before we catch the killer we could lock him up safely for a nice long time."

"Sergeant Kemp took his statement and threw him bodily out of the station."

"That sounds like Sid; he really hates men like that, like the rest of us."

"Here's his statement, go over it and see if there is anything in it that might help you nail this killer or killers, if the killer runs true to form Pearson will be dead by the end of the day."

"Did you notice who else is on the list Jack, Inspector Saunders we banged up, I did get a message to the prison warden who put him in a secure part of the prison. There are two more names on the list before his."

I read his statement, which claims a small boy climbed out of a pushchair a cloaked figure was pushing. The boy walked up to Simpson, fired a bolt into him with a small crossbow, climbed back into the pushchair and the cloaked figure calmly walked off down the street. I was confused because the dwarf was lying downstairs dead in the morgue.

I took the statement to my desk; something in it was trying to jump out at me. My subconscious had picked up on something and was being difficult.

I needed a bar of chocolate to help me concentrate but as I started to stand up a bar of chocolate dropped on my desk.

"I spotted you squeezing the top of your nose with your left hand; I keep a supply in my drawer."

"You're a little gem Carol, read this statement and tell me what you make of it."

"This must be a phoney? Terry Pearson would never come near a police station let alone volunteer to help us."

"No it's genuine, he is a very frightened man and I think it was the sight of a young boy killing someone in cold blood showed him how vulnerable he is."

"Shame he wasn't the first on the list, he even put women in hospital with his money lending, how about we sit on this till tomorrow then he will be out of the way, I would gladly wheel him to the morgue."

"That's it you found the clue you lovely clever woman."

"You've lost me what did I say."

"The wheels, do you remember the pawnbrokers CCTV footage of the woman and small boy looking in the window, because the wheels on her pushchair was different to the one we saw follow John Budd on the other side of the street we dismissed her from our investigations. Get the footage and put a name to her."

I decide to take our bulldozer Sergeant Green with me and visit Terry Pearson just to see if he could have mistaken the dwarf for a small boy."

I had to drop my identity card through his letterbox before he would answer it, he nearly shut it again when he spotted bulldozer towering above me.

I never told him he was on the list, in fact, he was not aware of its existence but he was aware of the criminals being hunted down.

"Mr Pearson the main reason we have called is the description you gave of the killer, could you have been mistaken about it being a boy, could it have been a dwarf. Is there anything else you can say about the cloaked figure pushing the pushchair?"

"I know the difference between a boy and a dwarf; I guess he must have been about six, as for the cloaked figure how am I supposed to see someone under a cloak, wait a moment! As the boy climbed out of the pushchair, the one in the cloak dropped their hands down by their sides. I'm sure their left hand had a big ring on it and it had a big yellow stone in it."

"That's very helpful and would you like Sergeant Green to stay here for a while just in case you need protection?"

"No I have this and I will use it so if that's all perhaps you can clear off."

"Not until you show us your licence for that revolver."

I couldn't believe it he had one, would I like to get my hands on the moron that issued it to him. We walked back to the car and drove round the block then parked up the road so we could see Pearson's front door. It was mid afternoon now and neither Bulldozer nor I was prepared to sit here until midnight. About six thirty a shot rang out, even from fifty yards up the road it was clear enough. We looked at each other in disbelief and within seconds I had driven to Pearson's house and we were knocking on his door. Sergeant Green wanted to kick his door in but when I pointed out Pearson may mistake him for the killer and shoot him he nodded and walked round to the side of the house.

"Chief quickly we're too late he's copped it the killer must have approached the house from the back."

I peered through the living room window and could see Pearson slumped in his armchair with a bolt sticking out of his chest.

"This is getting really embarrassing Sergeant better kick the door in while I phone the chief." As I phoned, I wondered how the killer managed to fire through glass with such accuracy, as I knew all his windows had been closed. When we entered the living room, I could see why and told me there was more than one involved?

A big breezeblock was lying just inside the window; one must have taken aim while the other smashed the window.

"Sir he is still alive call an ambulance, looks like it just missed his heart."

I carefully took the gun out of Pearson's hand and placed it in the sideboard drawer then went out of the back door to see if the killers had left any clues.

It would appear that Pearson had hit one of them as some blood was on the patio. If nothing else, it would seal the fate of the killer once the lab boys matched it with the killers, if we ever manage to catch them.

I went back in and Sergeant Green said that Pearson was coming round.

I can't repeat exactly what he said because it wouldn't be published but the jest of it was

"I got the tall one but I missed the little blighter" That is as polite as I can put it then he passed out again. I left Sergeant Green at the scene to wait for our crew and the ambulance. By this time, a crowd had gathered in the street.

Back at the station, I went directly to Inspector Forward to find out if she had put a name to the woman's face on the CCTV footage from the pawnbrokers.

No luck with that; although she was sure the other one that was with Harry Barrow when he and the dwarf Timmy Strong killed each other, was Barrows right hand man Tom Dyke. Carol had also found out the make and model of Dykes car. "I have his address Peter shall we go and bring him in."

"Have you forgotten he took Barrows gun from the scene and his name is not on the list so let's take an armed officer with us?"

We left with the armed officer and headed for Dyke's home, on the way Carol pulled over and pointed to a brown Ford Granada parked outside Garry Simpson's betting shop.

"I thought the betting shop was closed since Simpson's death Peter?"

"It should be, so what is he doing there? The solicitors have the only keys which means if he is inside he must have broken in."

An alleyway ran down the side of the shop and as we made our way towards the back of the building, we noticed an open window. The side door at the rear recessed in about four feet, I decided it would be safer for us to wait in there for Dyke to emerge from the building and grab him as he passed. We never had long to wait, as he drew level, Carol shot out and within seconds Tom Dyke was face down on the ground and handcuffed.

"She is more lethal than my gun sir, never would have imagined a lovely thing like Inspector Forward had it in her."

"She is full of surprises constable and by the way I'm courting her."

"Wow you are brave sir, you must have to think twice before speaking."

Carol pulled Dyke up and picked up the bag he was carrying. Once he was safely in the car, I looked in the bag, apart from a large amount of cash there was a book containing names and cash transactions.

"This could be the break we've been looking for, all the victims names are in here and a few not on the list."

"Peter do you think the killer is one of the names not on the hit list?"

"You could be right, on the other hand it could be the head of the drugs chain, perhaps the drugs squad are on to him and he's wiping out the chain and in doing so there is nothing to connect him."

"In that case we would have to take into custody the last remaining people on the hit list if we hope to catch him."

"That's the only way Carol, in fact it would be better to round up everyone in the book just to be on the safe side, call them suspects in a murder case."

As there were only four left on the hit list and five other names in the book it was worth the effort to try and catch the culprit?"

I had assigned two of the constables to try to track down the church Carl Jenkins had been visiting on a regular basis.

Once back at the station I called on Carol's computer expertise to gather the names of vicars running churches within a ten-mile radius of Tunbridge Wells. Once Carol had completed her search, we noticed none of the vicars names were in the book and none had been in trouble with the law. The only reference in the book that still eluded us was JT, which seemed to have been the organiser. I sat at my desk going repeatedly through the book, knowing something was staring me in the face. My concentration was broken by a thud on my desk as a bar of chocolate landed in front of me.

"If that doesn't help try praying, perhaps our vicar Julian Tap could help?"

"Carol you wonderful gorgeous genius, J.T. Julian Tap, he's the main one in the book and his church must be the one Carl Jenkins had been visiting, he gave Julie Black a false location of the church which led us on a wild goose chase, better recall the two constables."

"But the vicar was hit over the head and left in the cellar so who hit him."

"He knew the florist would tell us Carl Jenkins was not the real one and we would search the church and find him, giving him a perfect alibi."

"What if we hadn't looked for him and as the Dwarf Timmy Strong was dead, how could he escape seeing the cellar door and the room he was in was locked from the outside?"

"You're forgetting Tom Dyke he's not on the list and could be in with it. The keys to the room and cellar door were not in the locks so he probably had a spare and locked himself in."

"That makes sense but who is the woman? It must be Mrs Lextor because she left with the dwarf."

"Let's share this bar of chocolate and try to piece this case together, but first get Constable Arnold to pick up our notorious vicar."

Something else was playing on my mind and that was if our vicar only had a superficial wound why was he unconscious best part of the day. I phoned the hospital and talked to the doctor who examined him, he said he was concerned why the vicar was unconscious so long and ordered a blood test. The test showed that the vicar had taken sleeping tablets to make his self-inflicted injury believable. I asked the doctor if he had any news on the condition of MR Pearson, apparently he was dead on arrival at the hospital.

No one was aware of the fact that the killer was in the crowd and had finished Pearson off with another bolt; the ambulance men were unaware of the other bolt until they arrived at the hospital.

"That's another potential witness dead Carol Pearson is dead, the psycho with crossbow finished him off when they were putting him in the ambulance."

"We had better round up the others on the list and get them in protective custody before they wipe the rest out."

"Find out their addresses while I update the chief and get him to organise the roundup, once we have done that I want you to come with me and interview our only lead Tom Dyke."

Our chief Jack Taylor sprung into action, assigned officers to the task of rounding up the remaining names on the list, and insisted he headed the hunt.

Sergeant Reed in charge of the cells brought Tom Dyke to the interview room.

After turning on the recorder and announcing who was in the room etch I sat opposite Dyke beside Carol, my mind went blank for a couple of minutes figuring the best way to start.

"Mr Dyke so far I have held off as to what charges to book you on, I think you know why; you have a choice booked for murder or burglary the choice is yours, we need your help in identifying the killers and you need our help so talk or you could be the next body on a slab."

"You can't pin the murders on me you haven't got any evidence."

"Your spoils from the betting shop is all the proof a judge will need to implicate you as an accomplice, you will be an old man when you finally get out."

"I have never killed anyone and neither did Harry Barrow, I was late getting to the meeting in the woods and when I arrived Mr Barrow was dead and so was the little man; I think the little man killed Mr Barrow but I haven't a clue who killed the dwarf."

"We were under then impression Barrow shot the dwarf who's name was Timmy Strong and you took Barrows gun and Mr Strong's car."

"I arrived in my own car and I did take Mr Barrows gun for protection but his gun was still in his pocket and hadn't been fired."

"Whoever was with Timmy Strong let him kill Jenkins and Barrow then killed him, probably because he stood out in a crowd, he was most certainly the only true and loyal friend his murderer had."

"I took the book because my name may have been in it and the money was with it and Simpson was dead so my need was greater than his."

Carol went red in the face and leaned over the table towards Tom Dyke.

"Why did you think your name would be in the book if you weren't involved? I think you know who is behind these killings and if we chuck you out of the police station you will be joining little Timmy Strong shortly after."

"I think your right Inspector Forward release him and if he is still alive in a couple of days we can arrest him again."

"Wait! I can only tell you what I know and that's not a lot; the betting shop was a front for a drug consortium. I have never seen the one in charge but I I remember hearing Mr Barrow refer to them as ~blasted salty~ I think he was short changed on a deal and was also accused of creaming some drugs off the top of shipments to sell on the side by the one he referred to as Salty."

"Where does the vicar fit into the scheme of things and how many other churches are involved?"

"You've lost me, as far as I know they commandeered it for this shipment only."

"You must have some idea why someone has created this deadly list or have a good idea who is acting on it."

"Everyone on that list is the entire ring drug dealers but until you showed me the list I was not aware of its existence; the reason for killing them eludes me."

"What part did inspector Saunders play in all this? As you are probably aware he is in prison for blackmail and kidnapping."

"He's a really nasty bit of work and used his position to intimidate people and get rid of witnesses; I think he also used his position to cover up transporting the drugs between suppliers and dealers."

"Are you telling me he killed potential witnesses?"

"I don't think he killed any but he would plant drugs in their homes or cars then threaten them with prison."

"I have made a note of some names in the book you stole that are not on the hit list, are any of them involved in the drug ring and any idea who this J.T. is?"

"I am not sure but it could be Tanner, as for the other names I haven't a clue."

"Who is this Tanner? We have the impression he is the one running the drug ring, if you can finger him we may be able to get you a deal?"

"All I know he lives by the coast but that's all apart from he owns a boat, wait a minute his boat I must be a bit thick that's called salty. His first name is Jerry so that would match up with the J.T. in the book."

"Blast that's why we never clicked on, we spelt it Gerry instead of Jerry. I think I know who is behind the killings and why, as for you Mr Dyke I will put a good word in for you in fact I will go and see the chief now."

Carol followed me to see Jack Taylor the chief and update him.

"Hello chief we are sure we know the identities of the killers, Jerry Tanner is the ring leader and his sister Mrs Lextor and her husband apart from the late accomplice Timmy Strong they killed because he was a dwarf he stood out in a crowd so was a threat. We think if you look in Mr Lextor's grave you will find an empty coffin."

"Great work you two I will get every available man on tracking them down, as for digging up the grave we will wait until we arrest the others, he may be with them and save us the trouble, what made you two think he was still alive?"

"There was no record of a shooting either in the hospitals, mortuaries or police reports, thanks to Inspector Forward here we know Tanners address. We have Mr Dyke in the cells who was as far as we can work out, was the minder of the late Mr Barrows; he has been invaluable in giving us information. I am glad your sitting down because he claims the reason Inspector Saunders name was on the list was because his role in the rugs ring was to frame witnesses by planting drugs on them and threatening them with jail, he also used his position as a cloak to ferry drugs to the dealers." I thought Jack was going to explode as his face went red and his eyes looked like they were going to pop out his head.

   We were lucky in arresting the killers as we alerted the coast guard that a boat named ~SALTY~ was carrying drugs and was caught on their way towards the channel and towed back to our waiting arms.

Mr and Mrs Lextor and her brother were on board with two more boxes of church candles stuffed with drugs.

   It came to light that the woman with the roman nose was Mrs Lextor who was responsible for the murder of Timmy Strong but not until Strong had killed both Carl Jenkins and Harry Barrow. The ones that survived the list sang like a bird once they found out they were to be murdered.

Inspector Saunders or should I just call him Saunders will be an old man by the time he gets released but the three killers got life and in their case it means life.

   The Vicar Julian Tap was cleared of any involvement. He had been forced to swallow the sleeping pills, then struck on the head and dumped in the cellar.

The other names in the book were other bookies or just friends of Simpson.

Grace day sent my ring back with a letter that pulled on the heart strings but the feelings I had for her had been sucked out of my heart in a heartbeat. Carol and I decided we would have a long courtship, we attended constables White, and

Sky's engagement party, young love is a lovely thing.
Constable Arnold also announced his engagement to Nurse Langridge

Until the next case, stay lucky

Chief Inspector Peter Stewart

Printed in Poland
by Amazon Fulfillment
Poland Sp. z o.o., Wrocław

64074071R00074